RUN THE RISK

RISK

ALLISON
VAN DIEPEN

HARPER TEEN

An Imprint of HarperCollins Publishers

HarperTeen is an imprint of HarperCollins Publishers.

Run the Risk
Copyright © 2017 by Allison van Diepen
All rights reserved. Printed in the United States of America.
No part of this book may be used or reproduced in any manner whatsoever without written permission except in the case of brief quotations embodied in critical articles and reviews. For information address HarperCollins Children's Books, a division of HarperCollins Publishers, 195 Broadway, New York, NY 10007.
www.epicreads.com

Library of Congress Control Number: 2016958061
ISBN 978-0-06-243335-0

Typography by Ellice M. Lee
17 18 19 20 21   PC/LSCH   10 9 8 7 6 5 4 3 2 1
❖
First Edition

For Paul VanderGriendt

Tough as Nails

DÉJÀ VU

I SAW MATEO THE MOMENT he entered the movie theater's concession area, sensed him like a dog senses a tsunami.

Should I run for cover?

I turned away and focused on wiping powdered sugar off the counter. I'd never expected to see him again.

Feenix waved a hand in front of my face. "You okay, Grace? You see a ghost or something?"

He might as well be a ghost, because as far as I was concerned, the boy who'd been my first love was gone. I hadn't seen him in four years.

"Do you know the new security guy?" she asked, jabbing my waist.

"I used to." I grabbed a J-cloth and sprayed the counters.

It was almost time to close up the pretzel booth for the night.

Feenix looked him over. "He's damn juicy, if you ask me." She made a point of objectifying guys—it was part of her feminist role-reversal plan.

Back when I'd dated Mateo, she wouldn't have said that. He'd been tall and lanky then, with more than his fair share of acne. I'd seen past the acne, though—and what I saw was the cutest, smartest guy around.

He looked different now; the boy had turned into a man. His broad shoulders had filled out and his tanned arms were ripped, like he could do pull-ups without breaking a sweat. The dark ink of a tattoo peeked out from beneath his left sleeve. *Probably a gang tattoo*, I thought bitterly.

"Juicy or not, he's with Los Reyes," I said. "Or used to be."

Feenix's eyes widened, and I wished I could swallow back my words. The fact was, I had no idea what he'd been up to the last few years, and it wasn't fair to mess with his reputation on his first day.

"Luke wouldn't let any gang members work here—you know that," she said. "He can smell 'em a mile away."

It was true. Our boss was a former member of the Brothers-in-Arms biker gang, and he didn't put up with any gang drama among staff or customers. Luke was up front about the fact that he'd done time in his early twenties, but he'd cleaned up his act. Now he owned Cinema 1, one of the few successful independent movie theaters in Miami.

Feenix gave me a meaningful look. "Security Guy screwed you over, didn't he." It wasn't a question.

"It was a messy breakup, but I was like, fifteen. I can't even remember the details."

"We *all* remember when we were fifteen. But since Kenny's waiting, I'll give you a pass for now." She grabbed her velvet clutch and hugged me. "We'll talk tomorrow. Bye, sweets."

"Bye."

I couldn't take my eyes off Mateo as he walked the hallway past the theaters. Until now, I'd stayed partially hidden by the glass pretzel display. He might notice me anytime, so I'd better quit staring. But I couldn't. I'd always wondered what happened to him. My ears had perked whenever someone mentioned him, but it had been rare.

Here he was, in the flesh. I wasn't surprised that Luke thought he'd be good security. He definitely looked tough enough to scare the shit out of any troublemakers.

Maybe he wouldn't recognize me right away. I'd been dyeing my mousy brown hair blond recently. And he wasn't the only one who'd filled out.

His eyes scanned past me, then stopped dead. Question answered.

Uh-oh.

Should I smile or give him a *who cares* look? Unable to

decide, I looked away. My heart pounded in my chest. Out of the corner of my eye, I could see him starting to walk in my direction. Before he got too close, a customer stopped him to ask a question.

I grabbed a broom and swept the floor. Our concession was the smallest one at the theater, just a few square feet between the popcorn stand and the burrito bar. As I cleaned, I stayed low. I didn't want to talk to him. Not now. Not ever.

Mateo was a bruise that was still achingly sensitive when touched. Maybe it was because we'd never had real closure. Or maybe it was because we'd broken up just four months after Mom died. In my memory it was all wrapped together in a big, twisted knot of pain.

The knot of pain was in my closet now, in a box full of love notes and pictures. That's where I kept the promise ring. Just the thought of it made me want to gag. How stupid was I to believe that the promise ring meant we'd be together forever? That *I will always love you* meant just that. What a joke. I hadn't been mature enough to see that it was simply a horny sixteen-year-old guy talking.

Maybe Mateo caught my vibe, because he didn't approach me after all. Minutes later, I closed up the booth, dropped the register with Eddie, the assistant manager, and headed out into the night.

The sudden temperature change—from air-conditioning

to April heat—slapped me in the face. I took off my cardigan and slung it over my handbag, looking down at my phone. The bus was coming in four minutes. If I hurried across the parking lot, I should make it.

"Long time, huh?" said a voice behind me.

"Jesus!" I put a hand to my chest. Mateo had materialized at my elbow like a ghost.

"Sorry." His dark brown eyes were watchful. "You took off fast."

"Got a bus to catch." I did a double take. A scar slashed down his left cheek, from the corner of his eyebrow to his mouth. God, it was as if someone had tried to rip his face off. How the hell had that happened?

His eyes shuttered, and I felt bad for making my reaction so obvious.

I told myself not to feel sorry for him. He'd made the choice to join Los Reyes. I'd done everything I could to convince him not to. Getting hurt was part of the game.

I sped up, squelching the urge to run across the parking lot. He kept pace easily. "You should probably get back," I said. "I don't want Luke to think you're skipping out. He's a hard-ass, you know."

"Is he?"

"Yeah. Good guy, but a hard-ass. You full-time or part-time?"

"Twenty hours a week. Thursday night to Sunday night."

"That's all?"

"I'm in the paramedic program at Miami-Dade. I've got training shifts earlier in the week—seven at night till seven in the morning."

I blinked. I couldn't believe that *he* was in college and I wasn't. In what universe?

I bet he thought he was hot shit, too. "Paramedic, huh? Good for you." I didn't mean it to sound snarky, but that's how it came out. "Look, I've gotta run. My bus—" Just as I said it, the bus shot by.

"Shit!" I had the worst bus luck ever. Way too early or seconds too late. That was my life.

"Sorry if I slowed you down," he said with genuine regret. "I can drive you home. I'm due for a break."

"No thanks, it's fine." I kept walking toward the bus stop, then sat down on the bench inside the shelter and took out my phone. The best way to shut a guy down, in my experience, was to start texting.

He came into the bus shelter, his head almost touching the ceiling. It was just him and me and the dirt-streaked, graffiti-tagged walls around us. His nearness made my pulse pound and my armpits go slick. *All this time, and he still affects me, damn it.*

"Guess I'll see you tomorrow," he said.

I could feel his eyes on me, but I refused to look up. My throat felt dry. "Yep, see ya."

I held my breath, waiting for him to leave. Out of the corner of my eye, I saw him finally head back toward the theater. Only then did I exhale.

When I opened the door to my house an hour later, my stomach sank.

There were five guys in my living room, reeking of sweat and cologne. Pizza boxes, crumpled napkins, and beer cans littered the room. Did they have to be here tonight? Hadn't seeing Mateo shaken me up enough?

I shouldn't be surprised, though. Dad had left this afternoon to drive a load to the Northeast, and he'd be gone for two weeks—probably more if he visited his girlfriend in Atlanta.

"Hi," I said, but nobody looked up. They were all enthralled by a video game.

"Alex?" I said to my brother.

"Shhh!" He had a controller in his hand and waved me away. Alex looked like Mom's side of the family, the Hernandezes, but with Dad's blue eyes. His black hair was buzzed short with lightning bolts on the sides. He was five nine, but he had a seven-foot-tall chip on his shoulder.

7

Living with Alex was like living with a live wire. You tip-toed around it. Tried not to touch it because it just might spark and burn you.

Animale got off the couch and walked up to me. "Hey there, *hermana*. How's it going?"

"Fine," I said.

Animale was slightly shorter than me, and good-looking in a slick, disturbing way. Piercing green eyes raked over me, as if assessing my ripeness. He was the only one who ever bothered to talk to me—and I wished he hadn't.

"We'll take off when their game's finished," he said. "It could be a while, though. My boys here think they can make it to Level 13."

As if Level 13 meant anything to me. "He's got school tomorrow."

"Of course he does, Grace." He gestured as if there was a feast laid out. "We've got pizza and beer. Help yourself, honey."

I wanted to refuse the pizza as a matter of pride, but damn it, I was starving, and I knew the fridge was empty. I grabbed a middle slice—one their grubby hands hadn't touched, hopefully—and sat down on the couch.

I chewed slowly, too upset to actually taste the pizza. I'd told Alex so many times not to bring them here. But the moment Dad went out of town, they were back. As usual.

Alex had started hanging around with these guys almost a

year ago. I didn't like them on sight. Why would they want to hang out with my brother, who was several years younger than them? My instincts had been right. Alex had gone from a regular kid to a thug overnight. Although they never talked about it in front of me, I knew they were members of the Locos—the most violent gang around.

I hated them.

Last May, they'd all gotten arrested for armed robbery—no doubt Animale had masterminded it. The last two months of my senior year of high school had been turned upside down. With the stress of Alex's arrest, I'd had a bit of a breakdown. I didn't finish two term papers and failed three exams. It was a wonder I'd graduated at all. But my GPA had plummeted, and my acceptance to the Early Childhood Education program at Miami-Dade had been revoked.

After a few months of hell, the charges against them were dropped due to some legal loophole. I'd been left to pick up the pieces of my life—just like I had to pick up the mess they left whenever they came over.

As I finished the slice of pizza, I could feel Animale's eyes on me. I finally raised my head. His eyes sharpened. He saw the hatred on my face.

He had a tiny teardrop tattoo below his right eye. I always wondered if the teardrop was meant to represent his tears or other people's.

I held his gaze, telling him without words that I wasn't weak, that he wasn't welcome here, and that in the tug-of-war for my brother, I intended to win.

A smile pulled at his lips, revealing sharp incisors. For him, this was a game. Maybe even a turn-on. It made me sick.

I got up and went to the kitchen, cleaning up the dishes from this morning. When I finished, I took out my phone and killed time, waiting for them to leave. I never went to bed while they were here, no matter how late they stayed. I'd even thought about getting a lock for my bedroom door.

If Alex wanted to leave with them, I'd have to stop him. If he left with them now, there was no way he'd get up for school tomorrow. He was fifteen, for God's sake. School wasn't optional.

An hour later, I heard them getting ready to go.

I stood in the kitchen doorway as they filed out, eyes on Alex. He was sitting on the couch in the midst of the mess they'd made. A good sign. He wasn't leaving.

Animale was the last to step out the door. He gave me a slick smile. *"Hasta luego."*

I stared at him coldly. I hoped there wouldn't be a next time.

Once the door closed, I turned to Alex.

"I told you not to bring them here!"

He shrugged. "So? We needed someplace to hang tonight."

"Maybe they should get jobs instead of *hanging* all the time. That's what most people do."

His chin jutted. "I'm sick of you judging my friends."

"*Judging* them? They're the reason you almost got locked up! They're the reason I lost my college acceptance!"

He rolled his eyes. "Don't start with that again. Ain't their fault you couldn't keep your shit together."

I wanted to slap him. I didn't even know who he was anymore. He used to be a good kid.

"Animale's crazy," I said. "If you follow him, he's gonna ruin your life. I don't want to see you get arrested again or . . . or worse."

"Don't you dare talk shit about Animale," he said through gritted teeth. "He's awesome. The guy gets total respect wherever he goes. He ain't afraid of anyone or anything."

And that's a good thing? I wanted to say, but I bit my tongue. Alex looked up to Animale. He was his hero.

And there was nothing I could do about it.

DIVAS

"STAY STILL, OKAY?" I SAID, trying to hang on to the little girl's tiny toes the next morning at the day care. "We want them to look pretty."

Four-year-old Rosalina squirmed excitedly on her chair. "But it tickles, Gwace!"

Rosalina had been the most hyped-up of all the kids for Diva Day. She'd arrived this morning in a white bathrobe, flip-flops, and too-large sunglasses. She'd even said, "Hey, bitches!" as she strolled in the door, much to her mom's horror.

"We, um, don't say words like that here, Rosalina." I'd exchanged a glance with Kylie, and we stifled our laughter.

Diva Day was Kylie's idea, not mine. I'd organized last

week's Dance Party Day. I'd connected my iPod to a speaker and we shook our booties under a papier-mâché disco ball. When Kylie had suggested a Diva Day, I'd been doubtful. Painting preschoolers' nails was a challenge. First of all, their nails were absolutely tiny. Second of all, they couldn't sit still for more than five seconds.

But the enthusiasm in the room was totally worth it.

"How am I doing?" I lifted one of Rosalina's feet, showing Kylie my handiwork.

She looked up from Dasia's manicure and gave a nod. "Lovely. Don't forget your top coat."

"I wouldn't dare."

Kylie took aesthetics very seriously. Half-Thai, half-Jamaican, she loved the highest heels, the teeniest skirts, and the most glittering bling. When I'd first started volunteering at Compass, I might have judged her a little—who dressed like that to work at a day care? But it turned out she was great with kids, and dressing like that was just her thing. She'd even found a way to kneel down in short skirts without showing off her panties. True, some kids tried to yank her boobs from her ultralow tops, but that didn't bother her.

When I was done with Rosalina's toes, I sent her over to the carpet to choose a book. She waddled over. "Look at me, eveebody!" Kicking off the flip-flops, she started to dance around. That girl loved to dance even when there was no music on. Music, apparently, played in her head twenty-four seven.

"She's messing up her toes," Kylie grumbled.

"Oh well."

Working with kids was hilarious. And messy. And exhausting.

But we loved it.

My mom and I had both chosen caring professions. She'd been a support worker at a nursing home for twenty years until she got sick. Some of the seniors she'd worked with couldn't remember her from one day to the next. But she'd just say, *Love's never wasted.* Mom was wise that way.

I stretched, working out a kink in my neck. "Sofia, you're next."

The little girl looked up from her book, a mass of black hair hiding her face. She shook her head.

I walked over and sat down cross-legged, holding up my foot. "Do you like the turquoise on my toes? I also have pink, blue, peach, and . . . sprinkly, shiny cupcake!"

She frowned. "That's not a color."

"Silly me. That's just what I call it because it's got all different colors and some sparkles too. Want to come over and look at the bottle? It's really cool."

At first, she didn't move. But when I reached out for her hand, she placed it in mine. Sofia came to Compass last fall, just a week after I'd started volunteering here. As newbies we'd bonded, and I'd been her go-to buddy ever since. She hardly even made eye contact with the other staff.

At my station, she picked up the nail polish bottle, turning it upside down and back again like a snow globe, watching the sparkles flutter down.

"What do you think, Sof? Should we do one nail, then see if you'd like the rest painted?"

She put her hands in front of me tentatively, as if she might want to pull them back. Her nails were a mess—you could tell they'd chipped off rather than been cut. Although she was only four, she knew it was embarrassing, and the look on her face broke my heart.

"Let's soak them in water first to get your nails softened up. They're easier to paint that way. Then we'll cut them round like the moon. This is exciting!"

She didn't smile, but her eyes brightened, a ray of sunshine peeking out from the dark cloud of hair.

I didn't believe in playing favorites. But the reality was, some kids I liked, some kids drove me nuts, and some kids I simply *loved*, like Sofia. Life hadn't been easy for her. I got the impression that her mom was more focused on her boyfriends than on her daughter. Her mom had said from the beginning that Sofia was *no trouble, very independent.*

I didn't see it that way. I saw a girl who was lonely and sad. She rarely smiled like the other kids, and wanted nothing more than to fade into the woodwork.

But when she did smile, it was glorious.

"Wow, Sofia!" Yolanda said as she breezed by a few minutes later. "Beautiful nails!"

Yolanda Williamson was the beating heart that pumped life into this place. She wasn't the type of director who sat in her office all day. She actually worked with the kids. I loved Yolanda and everything she stood for. My dream was to be like her—to run a day care while teaching classes in Early Childhood Education.

When my college plan got screwed up last year, I'd spent the whole summer in a funk. Eventually I'd slapped some sense into myself. I wasn't a *sit on my ass, feel sorry for myself* person, was I? I was a *doer.* If I couldn't go to college in the fall, I had to think of something else. I'd decided to volunteer here four days a week. Not only would I be helping out Compass, I'd have more experience when I reapplied. I'd also redone a couple of courses to bring up my grades, and I just had one more class to go.

Everything happens for a reason, I told myself. If I were in college right now, I wouldn't be here with Sofia. She needed me to be with her.

And maybe I needed to be needed.

"First hand is done," I said. "What do you think, glitter girl?"

Sofia's soft smile hit me in the chest. "More."

No playing favorites. *Right.*

They say the human body can live without food for up to three weeks.

I couldn't live without caffeine for a day.

Just when my energy crashed after working all day at Compass, I ducked into Dunkin' Donuts to buy an extra large coffee with one cream and two sugars. Of course, by the time I got to the bus stop, I'd missed my bus.

This was typical.

After another fifteen minutes, I caught a bus to work. Cinema 1 was a four-screen theater that had opened in the 1940s. The decor was vintage—red carpet, velvet ropes, and brass—but the movies were not. You could always find the latest blockbusters here.

Luke was at the door, greeting moviegoers. He nodded at me as I came in. Although he had long, shaggy blond hair, he was often compared to Vin Diesel due to his big build and deep voice.

"Sorry I'm late," I said.

"It's all right." Since I'd been working here for almost two years, he knew about my life, and knew that some days I was coming straight from Compass. I hadn't been lying when I'd told Mateo that Luke was a hard-ass—he was—but he could be understanding, too.

I headed over to the pretzel booth. "Hey, girl," I said to Feenix, who was restocking the pretzel shelf.

She straightened up. Feenix was long and lean with a vine of thorny rose tattoos twirling down her right arm. She wore a small horseshoe nose ring, bright red lipstick, and no other makeup. She dual-majored in English Lit and Gender Studies at U of M and was a well-known slam poet on the Miami scene. People called her Feenix "the Fenom" with good reason.

"Hey, hon," Feenix said. "Mr. Security Guard's here tonight."

I rolled my eyes. "I don't need an update every time he shows up to work."

She raised her eyebrows.

"Sorry to bitch."

"I'm used to it. Means you need to eat." She used a gloved hand to grab me a jalapeño-cheese pretzel. "These are the freshest."

"Thanks." I dropped my stuff and took a bite, feeling the gnawing in my stomach ease.

Feenix served the next couple of customers while I ate, then we teamed up for the preshow rush. At twenty-one, she was only two years older than me, but she had the mom thing going on. We mom'ed each other, actually. We'd both lost our mothers—mine to cancer, hers to addiction. Although, according to Feenix, her mom's addiction was to men more than alcohol. She'd turned to alcohol to drown her sorrows over the men who'd used her up and thrown her out.

"We'll need more sugar," she said at one point. It was our secret code for customers with bad tattoos.

I glanced at the man's big, flabby white arms and spotted the offending tattoo: a long, curved eel with a cartoony happy face.

Ick! What was he thinking?

He wasn't thinking, he was drinking, Feenix would say. I didn't dare meet her eyes, or we'd both crack up.

After serving the customer, I rearranged some of the pretzels. I spotted Mateo through the glass, and my pulse kicked up.

"What can I get you?" I asked.

"Something sweet. Any ideas?"

Feenix made a strangled noise, and I shot her a look. He was just asking for a goddamn pretzel.

"We've got chocolate dipped, lemon and sugar, cinnamon, raspberry swirl."

Mateo looked over the display case, considering the options. I felt my cheeks heat up for no reason. Couldn't he choose already?

"Cinnamon."

I grabbed it with a glove, then rang it through with the other hand.

"Thanks." He paid me, then walked off. He moved slow and sexy, like a jaguar. I couldn't help but stare as he went.

"I can't believe you," Feenix said.

"What?"

"You didn't even ask him how he was doing. That's cold, Grace. Cold."

"Was it?" I hadn't meant to be cold. True, I hadn't meant to be warm either.

"What'd he do that was so bad? Let me guess—he dumped you?"

The customers had tapered off. There was no avoiding this.

"Not exactly. I dumped him. But only because he left me no choice."

"Ah, the reverse-dump. I understand." Her dark brown eyes were knowing. "He cheat on you?"

"No. Really, it was a long time ago."

"Looks like you're still pissed."

"I'm not. I'm over it."

"Maybe, but your cheeks are bright red. You got a fever, sweetheart?" Her eyes sparkled wickedly. "You need to get some, honey. You'll feel much better."

I sighed. "I'm not into random hookups, you know that."

"How about a not-so-random hookup?" She tapped her chin, glancing around the theater. "I have an idea."

I knew better than to trust her ideas.

"I say you hook up with your ex."

"Why would I do that?"

"Why wouldn't you? It would be a great way to turn the tables, don't you think? You could love him and leave him, baby. Full circle. Karma. Call it what you like."

Feenix was sick and tired of the way society screwed women over. It made for fierce poetry, that's for sure. Equal pay, gender discrimination, rape culture—she'd find an issue and skewer it, hanging it out to dry for all to see.

"There are so many things wrong with that idea. I don't know where to start."

"Ah, but the beauty of sleeping with your ex is that he doesn't add to your tally."

"My tally?"

She glared at me. "You know what I'm talking about. The tally of sexual partners by which society applauds men and shames women."

My tally was two. Ironically, Mateo wasn't even one of them. We'd held out not only because we were so young, but because back then, my virginity was something to be cherished. Guess the joke was on me, because that hadn't been the case for the two losers I'd actually slept with. I'd thought I was in relationships, only to discover I'd gotten with players who didn't know the meaning of the word.

"Can we change the topic?" I asked.

"Fine. But I can tell you're getting heated up at the thought, sweet cheeks. I say you burn it off through sex. Break free of the chains, baby!"

I pressed my hands to my cheeks, laughing.

Customers came up occasionally over the next hour, but it was near the nine o'clock show that things really picked up. Friday and Saturday nights were always busy, with masses of neighborhood kids out to see the latest blockbuster.

Feenix nudged me. "Something's starting in the lineup outside theater three."

I followed her eyes and saw two guys staring each other down. There was a tall, lean guy with tattoos everywhere but his face, and a thick, denim-wearing biker.

Puffed chests. Pride on the line. The international signs of a fight about to start.

"The Locos and the Brothers-in-Arms," Feenix whispered.

Those two gangs hated each other, and yet apparently

neither wanted to miss the first weekend of Dwayne Johnson's new action flick.

My stomach clenched. Where was Luke? I hadn't seen him in an hour or two. Usually his presence kept shady people in line, if it didn't scare them off completely.

Tattoo was up in Biker Guy's face. They were shouting at each other. Feenix grabbed my arm.

Tattoo shoved Biker Guy.

Biker Guy stumbled back, then took a swing at Tattoo, who leaped aside, dodging it. Biker Guy plowed forward, smashing him into the wall. Tattoo's head hit the wall with a thud that reverberated through the theater. The people in line screamed, running from the scene, stumbling over one another.

In a flash, Mateo rushed into the middle of the fight.

What the hell was he doing? He was security, not Superman. He didn't have a prayer of handling this without getting stomped. He should be calling 911—though I was sure there were at least two dozen people doing that right now.

Mateo grabbed Biker Guy's arm, deftly twisting it behind him and shoving him away from the other guy. Tattoo, who'd regained his senses, was frenzied now. He whipped something out of his waistband, and my heart stopped.

"Gun!" I shouted, though I was too far away for Mateo to hear.

But Mateo already knew. He ducked low, punching the

guy in the stomach, and used a karate chop to smash the gun from his hand. Tattoo grabbed his midsection and launched forward to grab the gun, but Mateo was quicker. He swept it up off the ground and smacked Tattoo over the head with it. Tattoo crumpled to the floor.

I blinked. How had Mateo learned to move that fast?

Four cops hurried into the theater. Mateo intercepted them, pointing out Tattoo on the floor. Biker Guy had already hightailed it out of there.

"I can't believe Mateo got in the middle of that!" I said, my pulse pounding. "He must be insane. The guy with the tattoos had a gun!"

"I didn't see it, but I'm not surprised. The Locos are hard-core." Feenix looked at me. "Insane or not, your ex is a freaking hero."

Luke thundered into the theater five minutes later, a storm cloud about to burst. Everyone stayed out of his way. He'd be furious that a gang fight had gone down in *his* theater. He prided himself on it being a safe place for young people and families to hang out—the type of place he'd never had as a kid.

It was just after nine, and the concession area was quiet now, except for the occasional boom of action scenes. There were two theaters full of people who probably had no clue about what had gone down. Those who'd been lined up for the Dwayne Johnson movie had mostly run out during the fight. A few had stuck around for the show, and some had come back once the coast was clear, asking for refunds or free passes.

Luke approached the last remaining cop, who was still talking with Mateo. Luke's face switched from anger to relief to anger again. I saw the exact moment Mateo told him about the gun because Luke went deadly still. His head dropped as he took in the fact that his theater had almost been the site of a shooting. He placed a hand on Mateo's shoulder.

Luke thanked the cop, then headed for his office. Mateo went back to his usual walk-around, his eyes extrasharp. Was he expecting one of the gang members to come back?

As the night wore on, Feenix and I weren't as chatty as usual. The fight had fazed us. When she went for break, Mateo came up to the pretzel booth. I couldn't help but think he'd planned it that way so he could talk to me alone.

Or maybe he just wanted a pretzel.

"Hey," he said, unsmiling. "You okay?"

"Am *I* okay? What about you? I saw the whole thing."

"I'm fine."

"You can't be fine. Some guy pulled a gun, and you . . .

Hulk-smashed him! Honestly, what were you thinking? He could've shot you!"

He blinked, as if my rant had surprised him. My face heated up. He must have thought I was crazy for going off on him when I should've been thanking him.

But then a light came into his eyes. He smiled crookedly, and my heart skipped a beat. "Guess that means you still care."

I scoffed and diverted my gaze, feeling exposed. "All I'm saying is that Luke doesn't pay you enough for you to put your life on the line. And what if that Loco guy comes back?"

"I'm not worried. He was too high to be holding grudges. He won't even remember who smacked him down. If he hadn't been high, he wouldn't have been stupid enough to pick the fight in the first place."

Relief spilled through me. Clearly Mateo knew what he was talking about.

I realized I didn't know the guy standing in front of me. I had no clue what he'd lived since he'd walked out of my life or how he'd learned to fight like that. Had the Reyes taught him?

There was a darkness in him now. I wondered if the scar on his face was matched by several more on the inside.

I had the urge to reach out to him—to know all the ways

that he'd changed. I was so damned curious it was killing me. But instead I said, "I guess you deserve a free pretzel for everything you did tonight."

His eyes glittered. "I'll take what I can get."

LIVE WIRE

WHEN I WALKED UP TO my house later that night, I was relieved to see lights on. Alex was home. And his Loco friends weren't there—even better.

I found him in the living room watching TV with a slice of leftover pizza and a glass of milk.

"Hey," I said.

"Hey." His eyes didn't veer from the TV. He might as well have said, *Go away.*

"I brought some pretzels. Day-old, but still chewy." I put the paper bag on the coffee table.

He nodded, like that was good news. Alex ate so much when he was home that I wondered if he ate at all when he was running the streets with his friends. He'd probably survived the last forty-eight hours on chips and soda.

"Drama at the theater tonight," I said. "Some Loco got into a fight with a biker. The Loco pulled a gun."

He looked up. A fight was sure to get his attention. "Oh yeah? Anybody get shot?"

"No, thank God. I can't believe that Loco was stupid enough to bring a gun to a movie theater. Think of what could've happened."

Alex shrugged, as if it had nothing to do with him. No matter how many times I'd confronted him, he still wouldn't admit that his friends were members of the Locos gang. My only hope was that he wasn't a full member yet. I'd heard it took a year or more to get past the rookie stage, and he didn't have the L tattoo yet.

"You wouldn't believe who smacked down the guy with the gun," I said.

"Your boss, what's his name?"

"No, not Luke. It was Mateo. He just got hired this week, doing security. You remember him?"

"Of course," he said, as if it was a dumb question. "So how'd he do the takedown?"

I explained the fight, the gut punch and the gun smack. Alex was riveted. "Mateo's always been pretty badass."

I remembered how he used to idolize Mateo, and sadness swept through me.

"Security's a cool job," Alex said, "getting to beat people down and shit."

"Well, it's just a temporary thing. Mateo's going to Miami-Dade to be a paramedic."

Alex thought about that. "I guess you learn to drive really fast and crazy, huh? And then you're the first on the scene after an accident with all the blood and carnage. Sounds freaky."

"You could do something like that if you wanted. I wonder what credits you'd need. I could ask Mateo for you."

"Don't waste your time." Any talk of school meant automatic shutdown. He looked at me suspiciously, as if I'd warmed him up just to bug him about school.

"The school called and said you cut the last three days," I told him.

He hissed out a breath. "I told you, if they call, tell 'em I'm sick."

"You know I can't do that."

"Why not?"

"If they think I'm lying for you, they're gonna call CPS. They've threatened to do that before."

"Who did?"

"Armstrong."

"She's a dumbass." He hated that dean so much. He hated them all. "You're nineteen. They can't mess with us."

"Who told you that—your *friend* Animale? I'm not your

legal guardian. Dad's the parent and he's gone half the time. I've been keeping that under wraps as much as I can, but they're wising up. Without Aunt Gloria looking in on us . . ." I sighed. Aunt Gloria and Uncle Baz had been there for us after Mom died. They'd lived around the corner up until a year ago, when they'd moved to Jacksonville for work. As much as I loved them, I couldn't help but think they'd been waiting for me to turn eighteen so they could move away. "CPS would never give me guardianship. No way."

"Why not?"

"Because you're always cutting school! If I can't make you go, that makes me an incompetent guardian. They'd be right, Alex. You don't listen to me."

He hung his head, as if he was actually thinking about this. As if he was actually *present* for this conversation. He waved his hand. "Fuck it." He grabbed the pretzels and milk and headed up to his bedroom.

"Leave me alone," he called over his shoulder in case I thought about following him upstairs.

I *was* an incompetent guardian. Hell, maybe I should be the one to call CPS on myself. Or go turn myself in, wrists out like I'd committed some crime. I wondered if Alex would be better off.

But I couldn't do that.

Dad would never stop trucking. Those roads were his

sanity. If CPS gave us trouble, Alex would get spooked, and might even run away. I couldn't let that happen.

I had to make sure he always had a home to come to. The fact that he still came home at all was a good sign. It meant I hadn't lost him to the Locos.

Not yet, anyway.

Before bed that night, I did something I never did. I opened the box.

Mateo had always folded his notes into cool shapes. I picked up a heart-shaped one.

Dear Grace,

Sometimes when I look at you, I have this weird feeling that I'm seeing you for the first time. It's like this flash—and it hits me that this beautiful, smart, amazing girl is actually my girlfriend. My Grace. I feel so damn proud.

My hands started to tremble, and I closed up the note. Why couldn't I throw all this stuff in the trash where it belonged?

I picked up the silver promise ring, glittering with its tiny diamond, and I couldn't help but think about the night we broke up.

"You have to get out of the gang," I'd said, closing my bedroom door. I didn't want Alex to hear what we were talking about.

Mateo stared at me. "Do you have any idea what Toro would do to me if I said I wanted out?"

El Toro was the leader of the local Reyes. From what Mateo had told me, he looked and behaved like the bull he was named for.

"If you keep doing deals for him, you'll get locked up," I said. "Isn't standing up to Toro better than that?"

"No." A bead of sweat slid down the side of his face.

My stomach tightened up. "I can't handle this." I curled up in a ball on my bed, hugging my knees to my chest. "I'm worried about you all the time. It's making me sick."

My stomach problems were nothing new. The doctors couldn't find anything wrong with me. They'd said it was probably anxiety manifesting in my gut. It made sense—the pain had started when Mom got sick. But it hadn't ended when she'd died. The grief at her death, and now my worries about Mateo, made me downright ill.

"I'm sorry, Grace. I don't ever want to hurt you."

I raised my head from my knees and looked up at him. Was he really sorry? Or did he just wish I'd stop complaining?

"I can't get out," he said quietly, almost to himself. "There's no way out."

"There's always a way."

He thought I lived in a fantasy world. But I couldn't accept that he was locked into the gang forever. He had a bright future—athletics, academics. He could go in any direction he wanted. If he stayed in the gang, he didn't have a future. How long before he was *arrested or even killed by a rival gang member?*

"Tell Mig you want out," I said. "Maybe he can talk to Toro for you."

His expression darkened. "You honestly think Mig would help me?"

Okay, so maybe he had a point. His big brother wasn't the answer. He was more likely the problem.

"I love you, Grace."

I looked up, hit by the sadness in his eyes. I could tell he was scared. Maybe I should've just said I loved him too.

But I didn't. Desperation took over. "If you love me, you'll find a way out."

His expression turned bleak. I knew I'd said the wrong thing. "I wish I could. But I told you, I've got no choice. I need you to under-stand that."

I stared at him. How could I understand it? How could I live with it?

"I can't." I shook my head, staring down at my knees. "I can't do this anymore."

He paused for a long moment. "You're breaking up with me."

I didn't look up to see his face. I didn't want to see it. "I have no choice."

The next sound was the slam of my bedroom door. I rolled over on my bed and cried. He was angry, of course. We loved each other. We'd made promises. He probably thought I was abandoning him when he needed me. But it wasn't my fault he'd joined Los Reyes. I couldn't stand by and watch Mateo lose himself to a gang.

The sharp pain of that moment jolted me back into the present. I wished I could black that night out of my memory. I hadn't wanted things to end that way. But in the next few days, Mateo hadn't shown up at school or returned my calls. Finally I'd gone over to his house and found him chilling on the porch with his gangbanger friends. He'd looked at me, dead-eyed, and told me to go home. I'd broken down in sobs on his lawn as his friends laughed at me.

I placed the ring back in the box and shoved it to the back of my closet, promising myself to never open it again.

THROWBACK

THE NEXT NIGHT, LUKE SPENT most of his time standing near the entrance, smiling and shaking hands. But he wasn't happy. Our numbers were down.

Word of the fight must've spread through the neighborhood. If people started associating Cinema 1 with gang fights, we were done. Over.

Luke wouldn't let that happen—and it started with manning the door. Mateo stood at the door too, and even frisked some guys as they came in. Mateo was an impressive-looking security guard; his scarred face definitely had a *don't mess with me* quality.

Still, seeing Mateo by the glass doors made me chew my

lip nervously. What if one of the Locos or Brothers-in-Arms wanted to do a drive-by?

But the night passed without incident, thank God. And despite Luke's mood, the party at his place was still on.

Good.

Saturday nights we always went to Luke's after work. I looked forward to it all week long. It was the one night that I could blow off steam—let go of all my worries and responsibilities and just have fun. There was always plenty of takeout and drinks there, though I could never let him see me drinking. I really needed to party tonight. I'd spent my entire Saturday working on a sociology paper for my online course. I'd already redone my twelfth-grade politics and English online in the fall, and this was my last course to finish. I *had to* get accepted into Miami-Dade again. I had to get my life back on track after Alex's drama had steered it off course.

As I sold pretzels, I couldn't help looking over at the front doors. Would Mateo come tonight?

Doubted it. He'd never been a partier anyway. In fact, whenever he'd agreed to go to a party with me, he'd ended up pulling me into a room so we could make out.

Heat poured over me at the memory. Did he think about those times too?

He'd always respected my boundaries. Never pushed me

further than I wanted to go. But damn, I wondered if he was still so passionate.

Must. Not. Think. About. It.

I thought about Feenix's idea to use him. Could I do something like that? Should I lure him into Luke's bedroom tonight, use him, then toss him out?

I wished.

After my shift was done, I hung around with Nina and Nyla Anderson at the burrito bar while Eddie, the assistant manager, collected and counted the tills. Nina and Nyla were twins who looked nothing alike. Nina was a tall, thin redhead with porcelain skin. Nyla was short and square-shaped with frizzy black hair and black eyes. It was to the point that everyone, even the twins themselves, speculated about whether they had different fathers. Apparently, it was medically possible. But it didn't say a lot about their mom.

Once Eddie was ready, we walked over to Luke's place. Feenix had already left, since she and Kenny were celebrating their anniversary tonight. I looked over my shoulder to see that Mateo was still manning the doors. I guess he'd be the last to leave.

I told myself not to worry. Mateo knew how to take care of himself.

Luke lived in a swanky building. Although the doorman was a little white-haired man who couldn't knock over a feather, he had the power to buzz us in. We rode the elevator up to the penthouse, and Eddie let us into the apartment.

Luke had the ultimate bachelor pad, worthy of a spread in *GQ* magazine. Everything was sleek and white except for a few splashes of art on the walls. His kitchen was all stainless steel and futuristic—there didn't even seem to be handles on the drawers. As usual, the place was spotless.

The apartment had floor-to-ceiling windows, and the view of Miami at night was breathtaking. While everybody dove into the liquor cabinet and Eddie called for takeout, I drank in the view.

What a sweet life it must be. Luke was twenty-seven and had truly made it. He had all the money he needed and didn't have to worry about anyone but himself. All I did was worry— about Alex, about college, about the next bill.

"You spaced out or what?" I heard from behind me.

Some guys would ask what I was thinking as I stared into the night. Eddie asked if I was spaced out. It was typical Eddie—he had a gift for saying odd things and for ranting about stuff nobody was interested in. He was twenty-five, skinny, with glasses and a soul patch. I'd heard that he'd quit college just shy of a degree because he was too lazy to take his last two classes.

"Not spaced, no. What'd you order? I'm starving."

"Chinese tonight. From a good place, too."

"Luke's feeling generous."

"Yeah, well, everybody held it down last night. He's still pissed at himself that he wasn't there when it happened."

"Poor guy."

I went over and turned the sound system on. It had taken me months to figure the thing out. Dance music blared out of it. With his biker past, I might've pegged Luke for a rock guy.

When the rest of the crew came in later, I felt myself tense up. Mateo was here. He'd taken off the security outfit, and simply wore jeans and a gray T-shirt. For a second, his shirt clung to his washboard abs.

Holy.

My eyes raked over him. Shoulders, face, ass, legs—he'd filled out in all the right places. Feenix would totally approve of this reverse objectification.

My mouth went dry, and I took a sip of my cranberry juice. Vodka and cranberry, of course. Luke wouldn't have to know.

Over by the sound system, Eddie and Nyla were debating about music.

"I'm telling you," Eddie said, "there's been no original music since the grunge movement of the early nineties."

Nyla frowned. "The *what* movement?"

"I take it you haven't studied music history." He rolled his eyes. "Haven't you heard of Pearl Jam? Nirvana? Stone Temple Pilots? They actually wrote music. Came up with *new* melodies. Now all you have is recycled beats and manufactured music. What we call rock now is actually pop. It's disgusting."

"That's so dumb," Nyla said. "There's totally been new music since then. The new Selena Gomez album—*hello!*"

Eddie pretended to gag. "Come on. All those pop artists—and it's a stretch to use the word *artist*—are Auto-Tuned to make their voices sound okay. Most pop songs out there are written by one of five producers."

"I don't have a problem with that as long as the music's good and it has an actual message."

Eddie looked like he wanted to shoot himself. "What's the message? Girls—be strong and don't put up with cheating douche bags, but make sure to look hot anyway? That's no message."

Eddie had a point, I had to admit. As I listened to the debate, I watched Mateo out of the corner of my eye. I saw him reach for a soda instead of a beer. Interesting. He'd always been pretty anti-alcohol, considering his older brother Mig was always getting trashed and getting into trouble. I guess that hadn't changed.

After a while, I ended up on the couch watching a rerun of *Ridiculousness.* Although the music was blaring, we didn't need to hear the TV to laugh our asses off at the videos.

Luke sat down next to me. I scooted a bit to give him room.

It felt a bit weird when he was so close. He was a good-looking guy, with his big muscles and the deep dimple in his chin, and I couldn't help but feel a ripple of attraction.

"I fucking love this show!" he said. Outside of work, Luke shed the role of boss like an itchy sweater. He was just a cool, sometimes even goofy guy, who loved dumb TV and girlie drinks.

When a commercial came on, Luke looked over at me. He was sipping a pink frothy cocktail. "How are ya, Grace? Things good?"

"Yeah." There was no point in spilling the beans about my brother. Saturday night wasn't the time for depressing talk.

"The day-care gig still going well?"

I nodded. "It's going great. This kid named Cameron has a crush on my friend Kylie. He trails her around all day. It's so cute."

At that, he smiled. "Watch out. Once the little player gets the vibe she's not interested, you'll be next."

Laughter erupted around us, and I saw a replay of a guy getting slammed in the crotch with a bowling ball. Luke went "Ow!"

I went to the bathroom, then made my way to the kitchen for another drink. Mateo was there talking to Eddie and Jamar, a college kid who worked the ticket line. Well, Eddie was doing most of the talking—he was ranting about the salaries of high-profile athletes. I poured myself another vodka and cranberry—light on the alcohol this time—to keep my buzz.

Before heading back to the couch, I asked Eddie, "Can I catch a ride later?" Usually I got a ride with Feenix and Kenny, but I'd gotten a ride with him a few times. The only problem was that he usually stayed really late. But a ride's a ride and I wasn't going to spend twenty bucks on a cab.

Eddie said sure, and I went back into the living room. My spot on the couch was taken, so I grabbed a kitchen chair and pulled it up near the others, enjoying the sweet tang of my drink.

Soon after, the TV went off and a few of us started dancing. Luke joined in and waved his hands in the air. I lost myself in the music. I was in that spot between sober and sloppy, where I could let my thoughts go and just feel the music. At some point I became aware that Mateo had entered the room.

As I danced, I had the feeling he was watching me. I looked over. A wild heat burned in his eyes but disappeared instantly. I must be imagining things. Mateo only looked bored.

If I was being honest with myself, I'd admit that I wanted to affect him the way he was affecting me. I'd admit that I wanted to stir up the same memories, the same need, the same . . . pain.

It suddenly hit me why Mateo's reappearance in my life had fazed me. He reminded me of everything I'd once had and lost. I'd had the most amazing mom in the world, a happy little brother, and a boyfriend I'd loved. It was a moment in time that would never happen again.

Once I'd danced myself out, I curled up on the loveseat and half dozed. It was still warm from whoever's butts had been sitting on it. I was done drinking, and the weight of the week was crashing over me. But I was on Eddie's schedule, and judging by the way he was rubbing up against Nina on the dance floor, it would be a while before I could go home. Sometimes I wondered why hot girls like Nina teased guys like Eddie. There was no way in hell she'd ever go for him, so why turn him on like that? Was it a pity thing?

But those thoughts were too deep for me right now.

Someone tapped my shoulder.

"I'm leaving," Mateo said, leaning over me. "I'll give you a ride." He followed my eyes to Eddie. "I don't think he's leaving anytime soon."

"Thanks." I wasn't stupid enough to pass up this chance to get home, even if it would be weird being alone with Mateo.

After letting Eddie know, we said good-bye to anyone who noticed and took the elevator down to the parking garage. I hated parking garages. They were crime scenes waiting to happen—or maybe I'd just watched too many violent shows. I shivered.

He noticed. "You cold?"

"No."

Mateo drove a black Mazda coupe—a sporty car, low to the ground, with no tricked-out rims or anything to draw attention to it. He pulled out of the garage and we headed down the I-95. No need to give him directions at least.

He switched the radio to WKTU, and I wondered if it was because he remembered it was my favorite station. It was strange, being this close to him after so long. I caught his scent—faint sweat and aftershave—and I had a flash of when he'd bike to my house on those hot summer days. He'd be dripping with sweat, a big smile on his face. I'd throw him a towel, bitch at him for not wearing a helmet, then I'd wrap my arms around him for a welcoming kiss.

Despite the music, the silence between us was uncomfortable. For me, anyway.

"How's your mom?" I asked. I hadn't met her many times, since I'd rarely hung out at his place, but I'd heard a lot about her. Mateo adored his mom.

He turned the music down. "Taking it day by day. I got a place of my own a couple years back, but I see her every week. Still works at Walmart. Photo lab now." He smirked. "Sees some weird shit."

"Oh yeah?"

"Old men underwear selfies are big now."

"Yuck! Your poor mom."

"Yeah, well. It's better than being a cashier." He glanced my way with a little smile. I felt a jolt of attraction and a sudden, spine-melting memory of what it felt like to have his lips on mine. Hoping he couldn't guess the direction of my thoughts, I turned to look out the window.

The silence was back, and even thicker this time, like a dense fog over dark roads.

"And Mig?" I said. "Still getting into trouble?"

"He's locked up."

"Oh." I shouldn't be surprised that Mateo's big brother had been locked up. Still, I felt bad for Mateo and his mom. "Sorry to hear that."

He shot me a glance, as if to say, *Are you really?*

I'd never liked his brother. I'd hated him, in fact, for pressuring Mateo to join the gang. It felt like we'd spent months fighting for Mateo—and Mig had won.

"How long's he in for?"

"Life. He has a chance of parole after twenty-five years."

I swore. "What'd he do?"

"He and his buddy Yellow had a plan to rob this lady. She'd been waiting in her car to pick up her daughter from dance class." His voice was stony, emotionless. "The lady ended up getting shot in the chest."

"Oh God."

"Mig said it was Yellow who pulled the trigger. He said killing her was never part of the plan. But you know what they did while she lay there bleeding out? They went to a club and spent the hundred and thirteen dollars from her purse."

The horror of it was overwhelming. I felt so sad for the lady who'd been shot, and for her daughter who'd never been picked up from dance class. Losing your mom was the worst—but losing her to violence was unimaginable.

Mateo and his mom were victims too. That's what he meant when he said she was *taking it day by day*. How did a mother recover from that?

She didn't.

A chill went through me. I pictured Alex in an orange jumpsuit, locked away. Would he get into the kind of trouble you could never come back from?

Mom had asked me to take care of Alex when she was gone. She knew Dad's limitations, and loved him in spite of them. But leaving her kids behind was the hardest part of dying young. I'd assured her I'd do everything possible for Alex.

But I was failing.

Mateo must've seen my face. "Didn't mean to upset you."

"It's fine. I'm the one who asked." I glanced at him. "You're not still with the Reyes, are you?"

"No. What was left of the Reyes disbanded a couple years ago. But I got out long before that."

"Glad to hear it." Mateo had told me that once you were in, there was no way to get out. I guess that hadn't been totally true. "When you dropped out of school, I had no idea what happened to you."

It was as if he'd fallen off the face of the earth. But I knew it meant he'd been swallowed up by the Reyes. They had become his world.

"That's all in the past," he said, obviously wanting to change the subject. "Heard you work with kids now."

Did that mean he'd been talking with someone about me? "Um, yeah, I volunteer at Compass. It's a Head Start program for kids whose families can't afford child care. Our director, Yolanda, is the real deal."

"I bet you dance for the kids. Bet you have big old dance parties."

I blushed. He'd so hit the mark. "It's called gross motor skills, and yeah, we do a lot of dancing."

"You're the only person I ever met who could dance while sitting down."

I couldn't keep the smile from my lips. "Dancing is in my blood, okay?"

"I never doubted it." He couldn't repress his smile either. "Remember the Halloween dance when you and your friends dressed up as characters from Monster High and performed that dance on the stage?"

"Yeah, I remember. I can't believe we did that. We took Halloween way too seriously back then."

"I thought it was awesome."

"You mean hilarious. Everybody pissed themselves laughing."

But the Monster High dance routine wasn't what I remembered most about that night—it was the night Mateo and I had kissed for the first time.

"Well, I was a freshman," I said. "You can't blame me for the lack of judgment."

"You were the most ballsy freshman at Rivera, from what I remember," he said, obviously amused. "You'd always threaten to kick my ass after school."

"I was just trying to get your attention."

"You had it, trust me. You used to come up to me and poke me in the stomach and say, *Your ass is mine, Lopez* or some shit like that. Remember that time you tried to get me in a head-lock and the principal walked by?"

"Yeah. He actually thought we were fighting. Talk about dense."

In typical freshman fashion, we'd had this flirtation going on, which came to a head at the Halloween dance. We'd both stopped to drink at the water fountain after dancing to a long set of hip-hop. We'd looked at each other, and had this moment where the world froze around us. Then we were kissing. Kissing with all the pent-up attraction we'd been holding inside. We hadn't stopped kissing for the next year.

"Those were good times," Mateo said, his voice husky in the darkness. I wondered if he was thinking about the same thing I was.

Our conversation dropped off after that. I looked out the window at the blackness beyond.

Eventually he parked in my driveway.

"Thanks for the ride," I said with a tired smile. "If it weren't for you, I'd still be waiting for Eddie to drive me home. And his car smells like he dropped a cologne bomb in it."

"No probs." His hand slid over the gearshift, grasping mine with a tightness that made my heart pound.

I looked at him, shocked.

"I hate to bring it up, but . . . you know the night you came to my place, after we broke up?"

My gut tightened. Did he have to bring that up, especially when we actually had a good vibe between us? I pulled my hand out of his grip. "I'm fine with you working with me, Mateo—it's not a big deal. But I'm not game for rehashing the past just so you can clear your conscience. Thanks again for the ride."

I slipped out of the car and hurried inside. I locked the door, as if to shut out what had just taken place. That was the thing about bringing up the past, I realized. You can't remember the good stuff without opening the door to the pain.

SLAMMED

EVERYONE HAD SOMETHING THEY DID for kicks. I liked to scare the shit out of myself, apparently.

Feenix put a hand on my shoulder. "Slam poetry is like throwing up. You always feel better afterward."

It was a good analogy since I actually felt like throwing up. I closed my eyes.

Feel the breath. Om.

This was all Feenix's fault. She kept saying that I had talent and she believed in me.

But did *I* believe in me?

Too late to question it now. It was my turn.

As I walked to the front of the café where the mike stood,

the audience clapped and whooped. I smiled, feeling the boost of their support. It was one of the things I loved about Oz Kafé's poetry slam: everybody wanted you to do well. There were no hecklers here.

I placed my sheet of paper on the music stand. I had the poem memorized, but I didn't trust myself not to blank out in front of the audience. I knew that if I held the paper, the faint tremble in my hand would make the paper shake. I'd done enough school presentations to know that putting the paper down was a must.

I cleared my throat and began,

You are all going to die.
At this very minute
The molecules in your body are quivering
Shaking, morphing
Dying with every breath you breathe.
It's inevitable, my friends.
The only choice you have is
At what point you put up your feet, wash your hands of this
Thing we call life
And let death unfold
Like an inky black
Welcome mat.

Then I looked up. The crowd was with me, wondering if there was more.

> *If you're lucky*
> *Death will write you a letter*
> *Promising to drop in*
> *When there's a spot in your schedule.*
> *The question is*
> *Do you invite her inside for tea*
> *White-haired and fur-cloaked?*
> *Or do you burn her words*
> *Her letter nothing but ashes*
> *Swirling*
> *Burning your fingers.*

I exhaled and glanced at Feenix, who grinned like I was her prized pupil.

Everybody clapped. I closed my eyes for a long second, feeling it. Letting in the love.

Feenix was right, of course. I did feel better. Lighter.

I headed to the back of the café, sitting down with Kenny at a corner table. He always showed up to support Feenix. He wore the usual sweater vest over a button-down shirt, fitted jeans, and a jaunty tan fedora—definitely looking the part of the poet's scholarly boyfriend. Too bad Feenix almost whopped his ass earlier when she caught him texting during someone's poem. He was careful to keep his phone tucked away now.

All of tonight's poets were good—each had their own unique style. When Feenix finally came on, I sat back and prepared to be wowed. You never knew what Feenix "the Fenom" would do. Would her poem be silly or downright devastating? Last week she'd gone up with a ukulele and sang a song called "My Paranoia" to the tune of "My Sharona." I hadn't even known she played the ukulele. But it was perfect.

"Hello," she said, and waited. Waited until she had us in the palm of her hand.

She placed her hands on her hips.

The Man Tells Me
I oughta get myself a husband
And pop out some 2.4 babies.

Spit-up gurgling.

The Man Tells Me
I'm no good unless I'm a something-mom
Soccer mom, hockey mom, dance mom.

Thumb sucking.

The Man Tells Me
My worth is in my children
In living for others, not myself.

Projectile vomiting.

Make no mistake
The Man Tells Me
That like in the old days
My worth is my apple pie.

Snot bubbling.

Well, Man, why don't you come and move
Into my ovaries
Work my job
Pay my bills
Whaddaya say?

Didn't think so.

She turned on her heel and abandoned the microphone. We all clapped. Some of us even stood up. It was definitely spiritual, watching someone do what they do best.

* * *

"I can't believe you're letting them do that," Kylie said.

Three days later, I sat in the dirt, covered in mud from the waist down. We were in the backyard of Compass, a huge umbrella shielding us from the late-morning sun. Little hands smeared globs of mud all over my legs.

The yard was filled with giggling.

"It's a mud spa treatment. My legs won't need moisturizing tonight." I looked her over. "Your knees are looking a bit ashy. Maybe you could use a patch treatment?"

She inched away. "Don't you dare give them ideas."

I grinned. I'd planned for this, of course. I wore a ratty T-shirt and shorts, and had another outfit to change into. Sometimes you just had to get down and dirty.

"You've gotta let them break the rules sometimes," I said. "They're less likely to misbehave if they can let loose occasionally."

"As long as they're letting loose on you, not me," Kylie said. "You're a superhero, Grace. I just think they should be flipping paying you."

"Don't remind me." Compass's paid staff all had to have Early Childhood Education certificates. I could've really used the money right about now. Dad had forgotten to pay the electric bill, despite my reminders. If he didn't pay it in the next twenty-four hours, the lights would go out. *Tick, tick, tick.*

For a brief moment there, as the kids giggled and globbed mud on my legs, I'd forgotten about my worries. They were back now.

Over the last few days, I'd felt a sadness I couldn't shake.

My Saturday night ride with Mateo had fazed me. Those moments of almost closeness in the car. The loneliness afterward. That feeling had stuck around, reminding me of the hole inside me that had never closed.

On the bright side, Alex had been going to school this week. That was huge. Although he still treated me like I had the plague, Friday night's conversation must have sunk in.

"You so yucky!" red-haired Mia said, laughing as she caked more mud onto my legs.

"You're right. I'm very yucky right now." I looked over at Sofia, who was watching from a few feet away. "Yucky is funny, hmm?"

She shrugged.

"Do you want to put mud on my legs? It's kind of silly, but I like being silly sometimes."

She looked like she half wanted to come forward, half wanted to run away. In the end, she tugged a lock of hair over her face and went to the other corner of the yard. Damn. In a group setting, it was tough to draw her out.

"Grace!" Yolanda brought the phone outside. "Call for you."

This couldn't be good. Nobody ever called me at work. Who even had this number?

Apologizing to the kids, I got up and walked over, globs of mud dropping as I went. I took the cordless phone. "Hello."

"This is Jennifer Armstrong from Rivera High School. I'm calling to tell you that Alex has been arrested."

My breath whooshed out. It felt like a punch in my gut. "Arrested? What?"

"Alex assaulted his classmate, Leon Benitez. I can't share all the details. There will be a court case should Leon choose to press charges."

Leon Benitez? No way. He'd been one of Alex's best friends before Alex had started hanging with the Locos. Leon was a loud mouth, but he meant well. I couldn't believe Alex would go after him.

"Is he all right?"

"Yes. He's at the police station on Second Avenue. You'll have to go get him."

"I—I meant Leon. Was he seriously hurt?"

"I told you, I'm not supposed to discuss the details. I'm just required to inform you that your brother is there."

"Okay. I'll go get him."

I heard her sigh on the other end of the line. "It's a real shame, you know."

What the hell was I supposed to say to that? "Yeah, it is." I hung up.

I closed my eyes, trying to keep a hold on my emotions. Just when I thought Alex might be getting it together—this.

I went over to Kylie. "Alex got arrested." I couldn't even believe the words coming out of my mouth. "I have to go to the police station."

She put a hand on my shoulder. "Oh, Grace, I'm really sorry. What'd he do?"

"I guess he assaulted someone." I couldn't bear to say that the someone had been one of his best friends.

"All right, well, I'll explain to Yolanda why you had to go."

I tried to put on a brave face for the kids as I hosed myself down, making a show of shivering as the cold water streamed down my legs. But it was all I could do not to cry.

Alex. Arrested. Again.

A while later, I walked up the steps of the police station, a red-brick building that resembled a prison. I went through security at the entrance, then headed down a hall and went up to a booth where I asked about my brother. I remembered the last time I'd been here—running in frantically, tears on my cheeks, asking anyone and everyone where Alex was and why he'd been arrested.

The officer at the booth directed me to the waiting room. An hour passed.

I hated waiting. I'd spent half my childhood in waiting rooms with my mom—mostly waiting to get bad news. Now I was waiting to hear what Alex had gotten himself into.

Alex could end up in juvie, where God knows what could happen to him. Or we could get sued for damages. Or, worst of all, he could face assault charges as an adult. I'd heard of that happening sometimes.

Just when I thought I would go insane from waiting, somebody called my name. I looked around. A tall black officer beckoned me. I followed him down a hall to a cubicle. Alex was there, handcuffed. He kept his eyes down, not even acknowledging me. But he had that rock-solid jaw twist that meant *proceed with caution*.

The officer didn't bother to introduce himself and he wore no name badge. "You can take your brother home. He's not being charged today."

I caught the emphasis on *today*. "But he still could be?"

"The victim has chosen not to give a statement at this time, so we can't proceed with pressing charges. However, he can change his mind."

"Is he in the hospital?" I asked.

"I understand he got stitches and was released."

"Stitches?" I turned to Alex. "What the hell did you do?"

"I didn't do nothing! I was defending myself. That bitch-ass Leon attacked me!"

You're a liar. But I wasn't stupid enough to say it in front of the cop. I knew Leon well—the kid had practically grown up at our house. He was a shit talker, but he wasn't a fighter. Alex used to tease him for being a pussy. No way I'd believe Leon had attacked him.

Alex lifted his cuffed hands toward the officer. "You gonna take these off or what?"

"When I'm ready." The cop leaned back in his chair with a sigh. "You might be getting off easy this time—depends on whether the kid decides to talk. But if you end up back here again, you'll get locked up for a good long while."

Alex scoffed. "I'm never coming back here."

"Oh yeah? Ninety-nine percent of the kids whose charges are dropped are back within six months. And the second time around, they aren't so lucky."

"I won't be one of them," Alex said. "I told you, I did nothing wrong."

"Right. Sure." The officer's eyes were jaded. "Keep telling yourself that when they make you bend and cough." He reached for the key to the handcuffs and unlocked them.

Alex got up, and so did I. The officer stayed in his chair. "Good luck," he said to me.

We headed to the bus stop. Alex walked all cocky, his face smug. Everything had gone his way. Instead of listening to the cop's warning, he was feeling untouchable.

On the bus ride home, I couldn't look at him. I didn't recognize my brother anymore. It was as if someone had stolen his soul and replaced it with ice.

Was this what my life was destined to be? Always coming to his aid when he screwed up? Part of me wanted to write him off. Stop trying to save him. If he was determined to fuck up his life, why stop him?

But he was only fifteen, I reminded myself. I'd learned in Bio class last year that the male brain kept growing and changing well into its twenties. He *could* wake up. Mom would never have given up on him. She'd want me to do everything possible to turn him around. Even if it meant standing up to thugs like Animale.

When we got home, Alex shut himself away in his room.

I could've taken a bus back to Compass, but I didn't feel like putting on a happy face. They could manage without me. So I watched some TV, then went to the grocery store to get a few things with the little money left in my account.

Later that afternoon, I decided to knock on Alex's door. "Can I come in?"

"No."

I opened the door anyway. He was sitting on his bed, texting. "Get out of here. I'm busy."

"You are? Well, I was busy too. I was at Compass when I got the call to come and get you. Do you know how humiliating it is to have to leave because my brother's been arrested? How do you think it makes me look?"

He waved a hand. "Tell them I'm not getting charged. It's all good."

"It's *not* all good. Why the hell would you go after Leon? He was your friend!"

Alex's lips tightened. "He was talking shit about me. He needed to learn some respect. I gotta say, Leon might be a pussy, but he ain't no snitch. I'm proud of him."

"I can't believe you hurt Leon. Are you crazy?"

"Of course I am." He smiled. "That's why we call ourselves Locos."

I stared at him. So he was finally admitting it. "Did one of your Locos buddies tell you to go after Leon?"

"My guys know how it is. If people don't give you respect, you gotta make them."

I gritted my teeth. "If you keep listening to them, you'll end up locked up. Didn't you hear a thing the cop said?"

He sneered. "All I know is, my boy Animale is right." He got up, looming over me, his hand grasping the door handle. "Sisters are naggy bitches."

"Why don't you tell Animale to come over and say it to my face?"

"Fuck *you*."

I jumped back as he slammed the door.

OUR LITTLE SECRET

"YOU'RE HUMAN," FEENIX COMFORTED ME that night at the theater. She could tell the minute I walked in that something was wrong, but we couldn't talk about it until after the first rush of customers. "Give yourself a break, Grace." She put an arm around me. "Maybe losing your shit is what it takes to wake him up."

I shook my head. "It won't. I know how his mind works. He thinks my life's purpose is to ruin his."

"That's fucked-up. He's the one who made you lose your college acceptance."

"Exactly!"

"You can use this, you know. Everything that pisses you off—stick it in your poetry and dump it on the stage."

"Nice imagery. That's what you do, right?"

She nodded. "Your last poem was amazing. What got you writing about death anyway?"

I shrugged. "Life. The wonder and the suckage."

"Speaking of the suckage, have your lights gone out yet?"

"No. I haven't heard from Dad. We've got until tomorrow to pay it."

"I wish I had the cash to help you out. You have to ask Luke to advance your pay."

Nerves balled in my stomach. I hadn't asked him for help since last year when my dad's absent-mindedness left us late on several bills. I'd gone to the Cash Stop a couple of times for an advance, but they took huge commissions. When I'd told Luke, he'd forbidden me from ever going to those "crook businesses" again, and said he would advance my check whenever I needed it.

"I really don't want to."

She glared at me. "That's pride talking."

"I know, but I don't want—"

She covered her ears. "Pride. Pride. Pr—"

"Fine. I'll ask him."

"Good. He's in his office right now. Perfect opportunity. Go on. *Go*." She pushed me out the swinging door of the pretzel booth.

Feenix was right. Unlike my problems with Alex, this was

a problem that could be solved.

Compared to Luke's perfect apartment, his office was small and cluttered. There were too many filing cabinets and a pyramid of paper on his desk. He claimed to know where everything was, but I wasn't sure I believed him. The walls held half a dozen pictures of Luke posing with celebrities who'd visited the theater. In here, he kept the minor celebs; the bigger ones, like Pitbull, Gloria and Emilio Estefan, and the mayor, were hung near the entrance.

Luke looked up from his desk and smiled. "Grace, what's up?" He waved me in, sipping a frothy macchiato.

"I'm sorry to ask this, but I was wondering if I could have an advance on my paycheck. We're behind on the electric bill."

His smile faded.

"Since we get paid Monday, it's just five days in advance," I said quickly.

"No problem. I'm happy to help you out. I'm just sorry you're in this situation again. How much?"

"The bill is ninety-six twenty, so a hundred would be good."

He opened his desk drawer and took some money from an envelope, counting it. "Here's one forty. A little extra in case something comes up in the next few days."

"Thanks." I carefully folded the money and put it deep into the pocket of my jeans. "I really appreciate it."

"Hey, I'm just lending you your own money. No big deal."

"It's a big deal to me. Thanks again." I turned to leave his office.

"Wait. Take a load off for a minute." He leaned back in his chair and gestured for me to sit. "Talk to me. How's your family?"

I sighed inwardly and sat down, knowing he expected more than some flip answer. "Dad's still trucking, long-haul mostly. The upside is that the money's better, but he's away for longer stints. He also found himself a girlfriend in Atlanta, so he spends time there too."

Luke gave a sympathetic nod. "When I was your age, I was pretty much on my own too. But I didn't take the high road like you. Had no work ethic. Was too damn stubborn to ask for help. Got involved with a group that offered me everything I wanted and more. I'm sure you remember where it led me."

Jail. I nodded.

"I'm just saying, anytime things get bad, let me know. If I can't help out people now and then, I'm a spoiled-ass jerk."

"Never. You earned your money. You deserve it."

He smiled. "I guess. Nothing was ever handed to me and nothing came easy. But here I am."

It was pretty incredible that he was so successful at his

age, and he knew it. "You should be in the '30 under 30.'"

He threw his head back and laughed. "I'd have no complaints." When he stopped laughing, his eyes lingered on my face for an extra beat.

I felt a twist of attraction. He was an undeniably hot guy, and you'd have to be a cold-blooded zombie not to notice.

"I'd better get back."

I headed to the pretzel booth and updated Feenix on the money. The late-show rush kept us busy, which was a good thing. Time went by faster.

Feenix left first, and it was my turn to stay the extra few minutes for the cleanup. As I was doing the counters, a text came up from Dad.

Paid the bill. Sorry for scare.

Seriously? After I'd spilled my guts to Luke, he pays the bill after all?

I wondered what I should do. Go see Luke and tell him it was for nothing? Or keep the money and not mention it?

I'd better give the money back. It would save him having to deduct it from my check. I wanted him to know that I would ask for an advance only when I really needed it.

Closing up the booth, I headed back to Luke's office. The

door was slightly ajar, so I gently knocked as I pushed it open.

Mateo was rifling around in Luke's desk. He stiffened, then closed the drawer.

"Luke said my pay stub was in there," he said casually. "Do you know where he keeps them?"

It was a good lie. If I hadn't known that Luke sent our pay stubs over email, I'd have believed it. But Mateo was too new to know that.

"We don't get paper pay stubs. What are you *really* doing?"

Our eyes locked.

He didn't blink. If this were a staring contest, he'd win.

Luke's petty-cash envelope came to mind. Why else would he be in Luke's office by himself?

"You're looking for cash, aren't you?"

Mateo's expression stayed blank.

Something inside me crumbled. Was *this* who Mateo had become? Someone who'd steal from his new boss?

Mateo circled the desk to stand in front of me. "We should talk about this."

"Since when is my office Party Central?" Luke asked us, arms crossed over his chest.

Mateo looked at me, a flash of fear in his eyes.

I handed Luke the curled bills from my pocket. "I was waiting for you to come back. My dad paid the bill an hour ago, so I don't need it. Thanks for helping me out."

Luke waved a hand. "Keep it. I already had Eddie deduct it from your pay. No harm, no foul."

I nodded. "Okay." To Mateo, I said, "Let's go. I'll chip in for gas."

We said good night to Luke and walked out of the office, then into the parking lot. I headed for the bus stop, but he touched my arm. "Come on. I'd better drive you. If he sees you at the bus stop . . ."

"Right. I get it."

We got into his car. Once we'd cleared the parking lot, I spun on him. "How could you? He's a good person. You can't just steal from him!"

"It was a bad call."

"A bad call? That's your defense? This isn't you, Mateo. You're not—" I broke off. *The guy I used to know. The guy I used to love.* Of course he wasn't.

"I owe you for covering for me."

Yeah, he owed me, all right. Why *had* I covered for him?

It was that look in his eyes, damn it. He didn't just look caught—he looked scared. The bleeding heart in me couldn't stand it.

"I haven't decided if I'm covering for you or not."

His head whipped my way. "But—"

"I didn't have time to think about it. Luke's a great boss.

He doesn't deserve to be disrespected like that."

"I wouldn't do it again, trust me."

"Trust you? The same way Luke trusts you?"

His hands tightened on the steering wheel. "You don't get it."

"Then make me."

"I need this job."

"So do I." I felt as if, by covering for Mateo, I'd been part of the crime.

But if I told Luke, he'd freak. He wouldn't just fire Mateo, he'd probably press charges. Even though, really, he wouldn't have much of a case against him when Mateo hadn't actually stolen anything. I had no intention of going to the cops and ratting him out.

Damn Mateo for putting me in this position.

We didn't speak for the rest of the drive. Before I knew it, we were parked in my driveway.

He cut the engine and turned to me. His face was grim, making his scar seem deeper, uglier. "So what are you gonna do?"

"I have to think about it."

"If you're gonna change your mind about covering for me, I need to know."

"You're not the one who should be making demands."

I saw a light turn on inside the living room. Alex was home. Yet another situation I wasn't looking forward to.

Then it hit me.

"I'll keep your secret on two conditions," I said, meeting his gaze.

His eyes narrowed suspiciously.

"You'll never try to steal from Luke again."

He crossed his heart. "Done. What's the other one?"

I looked at the light illuminating the living room. Part of me hesitated. It might be a bad idea. A total disaster. But the other part urged me to go for it. "My brother."

"What about him?"

"Alex is out of control—he's been arrested twice in the past year. He's hanging around with the Locos gang. There's this guy, Animale, who seems to be controlling him. Maybe you could help pull him away."

"Me? The kid probably doesn't even remember me."

"He does remember you. He always looked up to you." Mateo had been like a big brother to him. They'd played video games together, competed over who could eat the most chicken wings. Mateo had given him pep talks and taught him how to deal with bullies. He'd been the big brother to Alex that Mig had never been to him.

"Get to know him again," I said. "Tell him what it's like in college."

"Chances are, he'll want to know more about the Reyes than college."

"Actually . . . I never told him you joined."

He frowned. "You didn't?"

I looked down at my jeans, fingering the rip in the knee. "He worshipped the ground you walked on. If I told him, he would've been crushed."

He was quiet for a moment, taking this in. "If you really want me to do this, you'll have to let me tell him I used to be a Reyes." His expression was grim. "It won't sound pretty, and it won't sound badass. I promise you that."

"Okay then. Tell him what you want." I took a deep breath. "Just do this for me."

"Alex is a smart kid, you know. The second I show up, he'll figure out why."

"Depends how good of an actor you are. From what I saw tonight, you're real good. He'll think we're friends again. He already knows you got hired at Cinema 1. It's perfect timing."

Mateo searched my eyes. "If I do this, you won't say anything to Luke?"

I pressed a hand to my chest. "On my life."

He reached out, and we shook hands. The simple touch made warmth shoot up my arm, and I quickly pulled my hand back.

"You got a deal," he said. "When do we start?"

"Now."

* * *

Fifteen minutes later, I was in the kitchen grating cheese for nachos.

It was surreal.

Mateo sat in the living room, his long legs propped up on the coffee table. He and Alex were chatting about the Heat and their crappy new point guard.

The moment Mateo had walked through the door, Alex lit up. It was all I could do not to pump my fist. The hero worship was still there. It didn't hurt that I'd told him how Mateo had pistol-whipped a guy at the theater last week.

Smiling to myself, I spread half a bag of tortilla chips over a baking sheet. Next, the salsa, and some sliced olives from a can. I had nothing else to load them up with, so I covered them with lots of cheese.

I was taking my sweet time. No need to interrupt the conversation.

Mashing up an avocado, I made guacamole, sprinkling salt and pepper and a little lemon juice. I dumped the rest of the salsa into another bowl. I slid the nachos onto the top rack and turned on the oven light so I could watch the cheese melt. I was in no rush to go back in.

Creeping toward the kitchen door, I listened. They were still talking sports.

Good. Mateo wouldn't be stupid enough to bring up college, choices, gangs, or any of the things he'd eventually need to work into conversations. He had to take his time, build Alex's trust.

Build the bromance.

The conversation changed.

"So you and my sister, huh?" Alex said.

"Nah, it's not like that," Mateo said. "Been a long time since we hung out. We're just friends."

Alex scoffed.

I heard Mateo's laugh. "Back up. I didn't say I wasn't hoping to hit that. I'm just saying we can start out as friends. You know how girls are."

"I know all about it," Alex said, as if he were a seasoned player. "Sounds like you got a plan to reel her in."

Did I detect a note of protectiveness in Alex's voice?

"Yeah, truthfully, I do. I care about that girl. Always have. I wouldn't mess her around. You don't have to worry."

"Did I say I was? I don't care what you do with my sister. You and me, we're cool no matter what."

Mateo was playing Alex so perfectly. He'd been right that Alex wouldn't buy the *just friends* scenario. Better for Alex to think Mateo was trying to get with me.

Too bad it wasn't true.

Pushing that stupid thought aside, I carried in the nachos.

The guys chowed down, barely coming up for air. An odd sense of déjà vu came over me. It might've been a scene from our house years ago—except, back then, it would've been Mom making the nachos. Sadness rose in my chest, and settled again, in the quiet place in my heart where she still lived.

I studied Mateo beneath my lashes. Catching him stealing tonight had been a shock to my system. I'd known that he'd changed in four years—I'd already sensed a darkness in him that he hadn't had before. Stealing was a surprise, though. He'd always been a right-and-wrong, black-and-white type of guy.

But joining the gang had changed him.

It didn't matter who he was now, I told myself. All that mattered was that he could help Alex.

THE CATCH

"YOU'RE BLACKMAILING YOUR EX?" KYLIE grinned. "I like it."

We were in the yard behind Compass the next morning watching the kids play.

"What ith blackmail?" Noah lisped. He'd been building a sand castle at our feet.

Without missing a beat, Kylie leaned down and said, "It's when you get the mail back because you sent it to the wrong address."

He nodded.

I stifled a laugh. "Glad you approve of my plan."

"It's for the greater good. I saw your face when you got the call yesterday. Broke my heart."

The word *blackmail* sounded so awful. I felt bad about it . . . sort of. I didn't like that I was holding the threat of snitching over Mateo's head. But last night had gone so well that I wasn't going to backtrack. Mateo hadn't left until after I'd gone to bed. He and Alex had been playing a video game and chatting, just like old times, and they'd hardly noticed when I'd headed upstairs.

Mateo was Alex's only hope. Mine too, I realized. If Alex didn't straighten out, what sort of life was I going to have, dealing with the fallout of his screwups? He'd already thrown off my college plan. What next? If it took blackmailing Mateo to get Alex under control, so be it.

"Anyway," Kylie said, brushing a swirl of dark hair off her forehead. "It's not like Mateo did anything *that* bad. Swiping a few bucks isn't the end of the world."

"Thwiper no thwiping!" said Noah. "Thwiper no thwiping!"

"Awww man," I said, echoing the lines from *Dora*.

There were giggles all around.

Kylie wasn't laughing. "I'm a realist. You're doing what you have to do. If you think Mateo can help your little bro, then make him—especially if Alex is running with the Locos." She continued in a whisper. "They're the worst gang he could've got with. They have the neighborhood practically on lockdown. You look at one of their guys the wrong way and they come after you. Or worse, they target your family."

I nodded, not wanting her to say more. "I know all about them."

"What I'm saying is, if Mateo's the key to getting Alex out of this, don't go having a crisis of conscience. Make him help you."

"That's exactly what I'm doing." I knew Kylie would understand my situation. I wished I could say the same for Feenix. If I dared tell her about Mateo's attempt to steal from Luke, she'd probably march right up to Luke and tell him. She had a pretty strict moral code. I loved her for it, but I couldn't take the risk.

A popping sound rang out, startling us.

Kylie looked at me. "What the h—"

Another one. Was it a gunshot?

There was no time to think. When in doubt, treat it like an emergency.

"Time for popsicles!" I shouted. "Everybody inside! Let's go!" I hoped I didn't sound as panicked as I felt. Kylie and I hustled the kids toward the back door, pushing the stragglers along. Some of them paid no attention, and we scooped them up and carried them. Yolanda was at the door, grabbing kids and pulling them inside.

Another explosion of sound, closer this time. I ducked instinctively.

I spotted two kids across the yard making sand castles along the wooden fence that bordered the street. Adrenaline shot through me.

I ran to them. "Popsicle time! We have to hurry!" I lifted a kid with each arm and hauled them back toward the door.

I released them inside, and Kylie dead bolted the door behind me. We gasped for breath. While Kylie dealt with the kids, I ran to the front room to find that Yolanda had already drawn the curtains. "There's a situation on Flagler," Yolanda said. "We have to keep the kids at the back of the building, away from the windows."

I hurried to tell Kylie. Keeping sixteen kids in the mud-room wasn't going to be easy.

"You wanna be the one to tell them there are no popsi-cles?" Kylie asked me.

Gang-related shooting. A twenty-three-year-old guy was dead. That was all we got from the news that afternoon.

It had happened a block from the day care.

As I rode the bus to Cinema 1, I felt jittery. Of course, it might be the coffee I was drinking, but not entirely. Images kept going through my head of what could have happened.

What if the shooting had been closer? What if bullets had flown our way?

Screaming. Blood. Carnage. I didn't want to think about it.

I looked out the window, trying to focus on the fact that it had all turned out okay. For us, anyway. Not for the dead guy. We'd only been stuck in the mudroom for half an hour before we got the all clear from the police department. I should be grateful for that. The kids hadn't even realized anything was wrong except for the lack of popsicles. Thankfully we'd had bear-shaped graham cookies to give them instead.

When I got to work, I spotted Mateo near the entrance, standing below the huge Cinema 1 sign. He looked impressive and intimidating. Something fluttered in my chest. *He's a thief and you're blackmailing him,* I reminded myself. I'd be smart to cut off all residual feelings for him.

"Grace." He intercepted me before I could walk in. "I heard somebody got shot near the day care."

There was genuine concern in his eyes, and I had the ridiculous urge to burrow myself in his arms, to know the strength and warmth of his embrace again. Shaking it off, I said, "It was scary. We were outside when it happened. We managed to get the kids inside in probably thirty seconds. The news said a guy got killed."

"Yeah, I knew him."

"Was he a friend of yours?"

"No. He was a friend of Mig's."

I wanted to question him more, but Luke was walking toward us, and I didn't want to look like I was socializing when my shift had started two minutes ago.

"Tonight," I said. "You could come see Alex again."

Damn, it sounded like a request, but it wasn't meant to be optional.

"It's Friday night," Mateo said. "Think he'll be home?"

"With any luck, he will be." I didn't mention that my luck had been in short supply these days. "He's just as likely to stay out all night on a Monday as a Friday."

"All right, then."

I hurried toward the booth, surprised to see that Feenix wasn't already there. But Luke came up to me a minute later. "Feenix is going to be late. Got everything you need?"

"Yeah, I'll be fine."

"Good." He smiled. "Are you coming out tomorrow night? It's a special occasion, you know."

"Of course I'll be there. It's your birthday. Twenty-eight candles?"

"Yeah. You must think I'm old."

I shook my head. "You don't look old to me."

"That calls for a raise." He leaned on the counter, displaying a very pumped bicep. "So, did you give your dad hell?"

It took me a second to remember what he was talking about. "No. I'm just glad he paid the bill. Thanks again for helping me out. Sorry to be a pain."

"You're never that."

His hazel eyes were gentle. Under the big, buff exterior, Luke had a good heart, which just made me feel more horrible for not telling him about Mateo. But Luke was also a former biker and an ex-con—no amount of charm could hide that.

I glanced over at Mateo, who looked all strong and stoic in front of the glass doors. I knew I could never throw him to the wolf.

I just hoped he wouldn't figure that out.

Four hours later, Mateo took off his security vest and threw it in the backseat of his car. Sweat painted his navy T-shirt to his body. I swallowed and pretended not to notice.

"Let's hope Alex is home," I said as he pulled onto the road. "I think you made progress with him last night."

"You were right. The kid likes me."

"How late did you stay?"

"One thirty."

I should probably say sorry for that. But I wasn't sorry at all.

"Did he tell you anything about the Locos?"

"Yeah. He's hoping to become a full member soon."

"Oh God." I'd suspected that was the case, but hearing

him say it made it all too real. "How soon?"

"I don't know."

I inhaled, letting my breath out slowly. Meditation breathing: we taught it to the kids to calm them down. Too bad it never worked for me.

"I can't believe that he hasn't seen you in years, and he just told you! He never tells me anything."

"Of course he doesn't. He knows you'd freak." There was a flicker of compassion in his gaze. "He's proud of himself. He thinks being a Loco is a big accomplishment."

"How can he be so dumb?"

"If it makes any difference, it gave me an opening to tell him what I went through with Los Reyes."

"That's good. You joined when you were about his age. You two can relate on that."

"There's a difference, though. I wasn't given a choice."

"What do you mean? I know Mig pressured you, but—"

"If you weren't with them, you were against them," he said grimly. "That was their policy and they enforced it."

"You never told me that. You should've told me."

"I know. But I didn't want to scare you."

I stared at him. He'd let me believe that he'd wanted to join the Reyes—that Mig had made it sound like the coolest bunch of badasses ever. "Are you serious? I always wondered why you'd joined. Why you'd . . ." *thrown your life away.*

"I was trying to protect you." He looked at me. "I couldn't let you know the situation I was in. You'd been through enough already."

I wanted to reject what he was saying, but I recognized the ring of truth when I heard it. He'd always been protective of me.

"How long were you in the gang?"

"A year and a half. I went to juvie three months after I joined. Toro sent me on a sketchy deal. Turned out it was an undercover cop. I was lucky, though, getting put away."

I blinked. "Are you being sarcastic?"

"No. Two of the new recruits died in the six months I was in juvie. Fucking city murder rate was a lot higher when the Reyes were around. Toro didn't care that his recruits were dying. We were nothing but cannon fodder for him."

"You told me it was impossible to get out once they jumped you in." I'd begged him so many times. "So how'd you get out?"

"I stood up to Toro." His face turned bleak. "I had no choice. He was sending me on a job in cartel territory. I was sure it would get me killed. So I said no."

I was afraid to ask what happened next.

"They showed me what happens when you disrespect Toro."

He didn't give any more details, but my mind filled in the blanks. "Is that how you got the scar?"

"Yeah."

His own gang had done that to him—because he'd stuck up for himself and refused to be sent on a suicide mission. I swallowed the lump in my throat. God, I'd been too buried in my own pain to see the situation he'd been in.

"Once I got out of the hospital, they left me alone. So I was lucky there too."

"Do you think it was because of Mig?"

He scoffed. "Fuck no. Mig was there that night. Think he told them to go easy on his little brother?" His hands went white-knuckled on the wheel. "I guess Toro decided I'd earned my way out even though it almost killed me. He had a weird sense of justice that way."

"*Had?* Is he dead?"

"Yeah, he's dead. Most of the important Reyes are dead or locked up. First the Destinos went after them. Then a Mexican cartel finished them off."

"Did Mig ever try to get out of the gang?"

"Why would he? He was a lifer in the gang. Now he's a lifer in prison." He slowed the car, braking at a stop light. "He writes to me and Mom every week, going on about prison and how shitty it is. Was he stupid enough to think he'd end up anyplace else?"

He didn't seem to be expecting an answer because he went

on, "Mom keeps bugging me to write him back. But I've got nothing to say to him."

When he pulled into my driveway, the lights in my house were out. Damn it. I needed Alex to be home tonight. I needed him safe. This morning's gunshots rang in my ears.

Cutting the engine, Mateo took out his phone.

I saw him type: At your place. Where are you?

"He gave you his number?"

"Sure. I sent him a link to a Grand Theft Auto fan site this morning."

"Did he answer you?"

"Yeah. He thanked me."

Alex's response came up. Chillin with my bros.

"Offer to pick him up," I said.

Mateo shook his head. "Too obvious."

I looked over Mateo's shoulder as he typed: Have fun. Better knock before you come in 'cause I hope to be hitting it with your sis.

He sent the message before I could stop him. I smacked his arm. "What the hell?"

Mateo turned to me, and our faces were too close. His eyes drifted over my face and came to rest on my mouth.

There'd been a time when I'd have yanked his head over to mine, tangled my hands in his hair, and teased him with my tongue. His breath would catch, and I'd sense how turned on he was.

"I gotta play it real," he said softly. "He's not dumb enough to think we'd be friends. He wouldn't even respect me if he thought I wasn't trying to get with you." He broke off, shifting in his seat, avoiding my eyes.

"Fine." I took off my seat belt but didn't move. "Just promise me one thing. Promise me you'll keep him from becoming a full member of the gang."

"I'll try. That's all I can tell you."

I didn't want him to *try*. I wanted him to come through for me. I wanted him to make up for walking out of Alex's life—and mine—when he could've made a difference.

"Don't just try. Do whatever you have to."

He slanted me a look. "You sure about that?"

"I'm sure. You're gonna have to think of something. Because if he joins—" I broke off. I had to let Mateo know exactly how serious I was. "If he joins, I'll tell Luke everything."

I started to open the door, but in a split second, Mateo reached across the car and grabbed my arm. An electric current shot through me.

"Don't do that, Grace. Don't threaten me."

"But—"

"Believe it or not, I give a fuck about your brother. I don't want him to go through what I did. I don't want him to end up like Mig."

I smiled tightly. "Good. Then prove it." I got out of the car and slammed the door.

RECON

AT ELEVEN O'CLOCK THE NEXT night, I swayed on the dance floor, drink in hand. The lights of the club dipped and intersected. Hard beats pumped through my blood as I moved. Next to me, Feenix danced like her life depended on it. That girl could work it like an NFL cheerleader.

I didn't know how I'd gotten in here, except that when Luke strolled in with us, the doorman didn't check our IDs. Luke must've known him, because even with ID, it wasn't an easy club to get into.

Luke was in the center of the dance floor, sort of dancing as guys did, with a bunch of us dancing around him. A dozen other friends of his had shown up, mostly hot girls, all of them vying for his attention. Must be nice, I thought, picturing what it would be like to have a bunch of hot guys all over me.

In what universe?

Anyway, I was happy to enjoy my drink and dance. When I was dancing, nothing could touch me.

Well, almost nothing. Mateo was leaning on the bar, carelessly sexy in jeans and a black button-down shirt. A gold chain glittered on his neck. I couldn't help tracking his movements. He was standing with Eddie, who was talking and waving his arms, no doubt going on about the evils of pop music. Mateo didn't seem to be paying him much attention.

I was surprised that he'd come out to the club. It seemed a little hypocritical to try to steal from someone, then attend his birthday party.

A Miley Cyrus song came on, and suddenly there was a lot of twerking going on around me. Nina and Nyla were into it. There was something so wrong about two sisters putting on a twerking show. Feenix stopped dancing, looking around in disgust at what she called PP—prehistoric posturing. As a joke, some of the guys started twerking too. I figured I'd join in. Everybody was either twerking or laughing at that point. Even Feenix gave up and laughed.

Mateo was watching all of this. He wasn't amused.

Why are you even here? I wanted to ask him.

Was he keeping an eye on me? Was he worried I'd get drunk and tell Luke about his stealing attempt?

Of course he was worried. I'd made sure of it.

Oh well. I turned my back to him and kept dancing.

It's a known fact that you have to jump up and down when your favorite artist comes on. For me, that was Pitbull. Our love of Pitbull was one of the few nonbiological things Alex and I had in common.

"Woohoo!" Feenix and I yelled.

I felt hands on my hips, and looked over my shoulder to see Luke dancing behind me. He leaned down to my ear. "Always think of you when Pitbull comes on."

My Pitbull obsession was sort of a joke at work. I played it up by blowing kisses at his picture when I walked by.

"I told you I was gonna marry him, didn't I?" I said over my shoulder, feeling his fingers digging into my hips. I was very aware that I was extremely close to him. That if I shook my ass a little too much, I'd be rubbing into him. That felt dangerous.

But it was nothing compared to the look on Mateo's face as he watched us from across the dance floor.

What did he care?

As the dance ended, I eased away, then felt Luke's arms go around me in a hug. My boobs pressed against his chest, and I admit that I felt tingly all over. I couldn't help it. The guy wore sex on his sleeve.

"Thanks for coming tonight," Luke said, and before I could reply, he was grabbed back by his ladies.

I made a quick pee stop. When I walked out of the bathroom, Mateo was there.

"Hey," I said, startled.

He didn't say anything. He gently pulled me out of the way so a couple of girls could get by.

"Do you have an update for me?" I asked. "Alex never came home last night."

"I know. We've been in touch, but I don't know exactly where he is."

Mateo was looking down at me, and I realized his hands were still gripping my arms—not too tight, but not easy to slip out of either. Not that I wanted to move away. He had me up against the wall. The pull between us was so strong that I couldn't meet his eyes—because he'd know what I was feeling.

"Did he say when he'll be coming home?"

"No. I'm working on it."

I glanced up. He looked sort of angry. I wasn't surprised, considering the way I'd threatened him last night.

"Getting close to Luke is a bad idea," he said.

The change of topic startled me. "Come on. Do you honestly think I want Luke? I mean, he's, um, kind of hot, but . . ."

"I think he wants you."

"Whatever. Luke's a good guy, but I know what he is."

He didn't look reassured. "I hope so."

"What do you have against him, anyway?"

He frowned. "What do you mean?"

"You don't steal from just anyone, right? I figure it's only people you don't like. Or maybe I'm wrong."

"You're wrong. And I don't have a secret drug problem, and I don't owe anybody money, in case you're wondering. You can put it down to a crime of opportunity."

There was a time when I'd believed everything Mateo said. He'd been one of the most honest people I knew, and I'd never had any reason to doubt him. Sometimes he'd tell me the truth even if it wasn't what I wanted to hear. But now, I didn't know if he was telling the truth. I doubted he was that honest-to-a-fault guy anymore.

He leaned down suddenly, and my breath caught. His lips were inches from mine. It would be so easy, so natural, to kiss him. My mind might be all twisted up with confusion, but my body wasn't. My body remembered everything about him. His touch. His scent. His taste.

I looked at his mouth and wet my lips instinctively.

I didn't know what I'd do if he kissed me. Okay, I did. I'd kiss him back. I'd revel in this hot vibe between us, if only for a couple of minutes, then I'd push him away to let him know he wasn't going to get any more than that.

But he wasn't trying to kiss me. He was just hovering there. It was like his whole body had frozen into robot mode, and he was waiting for me to do something, press some button, to put him into motion.

"Well?" I asked.

"Sorry." He blinked. "Just having flashbacks, if you know what I mean."

God, I knew exactly what he meant. Flashbacks to those nights we'd been all over each other, almost crazed with wanting each other. Sometimes I wish we'd done it—had sex. He should've been my first. Maybe if I'd slept with him, I could've rid myself of him. Could've filled the need. Maybe then I wouldn't still want him.

"Remember the party at Rita's house?" he asked huskily.

I felt all my lower muscles tighten. I would never forget that night. We'd made out till dawn, straining together, crossing lines we hadn't intended to cross. "I remember."

His lips moved in a wicked smile. "Me too."

"No amount of concealer can save you, girl," Kylie said at the mall the next day.

Shopping the makeup section wasn't a good idea after a

sleepless night. The sinkholes under my eyes looked ready to swallow my face.

Kylie, of course, looked bright and shiny. "Big night last night?"

"Yes and no." I'd caught a ride home with Feenix and Kenny around one a.m., but hadn't been able to sleep. I kept waiting, hoping, for Alex to walk in the door. But he never did. So I just stared at the ceiling, mind wandering.

After my encounter with Mateo at the club, I was just a little revved up.

"Alex didn't come home again last night," I said, dabbing at a lipstick sample and smearing it on the back of my hand.

"That color's too dark for you." She looked at me. "I hope you're still on Mateo's case."

"Oh yeah." I showed her the text I sent him this morning.

Please text Alex and tell him if he's not home by 10
tonight I'm gonna find him and drag his ass home.

His reply: OK.

Kylie looked skeptical. "Are you sure you want to give Alex an ultimatum? He'll know you're bluffing."

"I'm not bluffing."

She raised her eyebrows. "Oh really? So what are you gonna do come ten o'clock? Walk the streets calling his name like he's a lost pet?"

"Something like that. I'll ask around. Find out where he is."

"It's a bad idea." She took a sip of her iced mocha before turning to the selection of lip glosses.

"Do you have a better one?"

"No, but I can spot a bad one a mile away. You know I tell you the truth, right?"

"Yes. That's why I love you so much."

She pouted into the mirror, checking her face. "Love you too, baby. Tell me, what if you find him? Are you going to yank him home by the ear in front of a bunch of Locos?"

"I haven't figured that part out yet."

"Promise me you won't go out looking for him."

"I can't. What would you do if he were your brother?"

"Honestly? I have no clue. But I do know I wouldn't go on some late-night recon mission."

"I have to do *something*. I keep feeling like time's running out, like something bad is going to happen to him."

Her eyes widened. "Where do you have this feeling?"

"*Where* do I feel it?" It was a strange question, but right away my hand went to my gut. It was where I felt everything.

Kylie bit her lip. "Yikes. My grandma used to say, if you feel it in your head, ignore it. If you feel it in your gut, don't you dare."

"I bet your grandma would support me going to find him."

"She'd support you calling the police, reporting him missing."

"If I do that, he'll be so pissed he'll run away as soon as he gets the chance."

"You could have the school do it. Or your dad."

I shook my head. "It doesn't matter who does it. He'll take it as an attack on his freedom. You know what he's like."

"Have you thought about ratting out your dad for being gone so much? Mr. No Show?"

Kylie didn't like my dad. Not for anything he'd actually done, but for everything he hadn't. As far as I was concerned, Dad was like a kid, too absorbed by his own needs to really see anyone else's. I couldn't hate him for letting us down when he was too clueless to realize it.

When Mom had gotten sick, Dad was around even less than usual. He seemed to take on more cross-country routes than ever. Medical bills, he'd said—and it was partly true. But we all knew it was his escape. *He can't handle how he feels, so he runs*, Mom once said.

Not all men were like that, though. Kylie's dad wasn't. He was a teddy bear who cried at TV shows and gave her roses before her prom. She was a daddy's girl, through and through.

"I called Dad this morning and told him Alex didn't come home again last night. He promised he wouldn't be away too long this time. But I can't wait on Dad to go chasing after Alex. Mateo told me that he isn't a full-fledged member of the Locos yet. But they could initiate him any day."

She sighed. "Fine. If you insist on going into gang territory in the middle of the night, you'll need a ride. Call me tonight."

"It's okay. Mateo's going with me."

She raised her eyebrows. "Has he agreed to this?"

I shrugged. "Does it matter?"

"You're badass, girl."

That night, at ten fifteen, Mateo and I sat in my driveway.

We'd barely said two words to each other on the ride home. The lights in the house were out. Alex obviously hadn't taken my threat seriously.

"He never replied to my text," Mateo said after checking his phone.

"Then we have to go find him. I hope you knew I was serious."

His eyes flickered with the faintest amusement. "Never doubted it."

"Will you drive me?"

"Hell yeah. I'm not gonna let you go by yourself."

Well, that was easier than expected. "Where should we start?"

"I have an idea. But I want you to understand, we have to be real careful here. At best we piss off Alex. At worst we piss off the Locos."

"So? They've pissed me off."

"When you get pissed off, you don't shoot people. That's the difference. I want you to promise that you're gonna let me handle this."

"Fine. I promise."

He looked down at his phone, writing a text. He showed it to me.

Heads up. Sis on a rampage looking for you. Let me
know where you're at.

"What are you doing? If you think you know where we can find him, why tip him off?"

"It's about saving face." He sent the text. "This is how we're gonna get him home. Not by taking him by surprise."

He drove to a sketchy neighborhood ten minutes away. Housing projects were crammed together, block after block, the exteriors peeling and dilapidated. While at first the neighborhood seemed deserted, I gradually spotted clusters of people on balconies, doorsteps, and between houses. They watched us drive by as if they knew, by the sight of an unfamiliar car, that we didn't belong.

One brave deli had a neon Open sign, but several other strip-mall businesses had been boarded up for good. Mateo pulled over near the deli but didn't turn off the engine. A text came up on his phone. He showed me.

Tell her to chill the fuck out.

Mateo swore. "Your brother's a pain in the ass."

"And so am I?"

He looked at me meaningfully. "You're something else altogether." He texted Alex: We're here. Come out with your hands up. Lol. Seriously you better come with us if you don't want drama.

"Let's go," he said, getting out of the car.

Eyes followed us as we walked down the street. I was no fragile flower, but I didn't feel safe here. I stayed close by Mateo's side, reminding myself that this was a good idea. I had to prove to Alex that I wasn't bluffing. He couldn't just do whatever he wanted.

"Where are we going?" I asked.

"Animale's house."

My stomach tensed. "How do you know where he lives?"

"The guy's hooked up from his ears to his ass. Doesn't go

anywhere without snapping a picture. Thinks he's a gangsta celeb or something. I saw enough on his pages to know where he lives. Anyway, it's a place to start."

"Good idea. I should've thought of that. Alex blocked me from his Facebook page, so I had to create a fake profile just to see it." I brought the page up on my phone and showed him Kylie's picture.

"Alexandra Chen. Nice."

"I wish I didn't have to do it. These are pictures of my friend Kylie who works at Compass—with her permission, of course."

"Of course." He seemed to be restraining a smile.

"I posted a few pictures initially to make the profile look real, but then I started getting all these friend requests from random guys. It was nonstop."

Now he was laughing. "So what'd you do?"

"I had to set the profile to private. That's what Kylie had to do with her own profile. It's not easy being that hot, apparently."

"Not a problem I've had. I've got to say, I'm impressed." His eyes twinkled. "You're shady when you want to be."

"Should I be flattered?"

"Absolutely." His smile made my breath catch.

Mateo suddenly stopped walking.

"That's the place over there," he said.

It was a small, run-down white house. A group of guys chilled on the porch. Well, maybe *chilled* wasn't the right word. They seemed too serious—especially the tall, heavily tattooed guy whose legs were propped up on the table. He looked older than the others. I recognized him from somewhere.

"Wait here," Mateo said, stopping me at the curb.

"But—"

"You promised."

"Frigging all right."

He approached the front steps but didn't climb them. He placed a hand over the chipped white banister. "Hey, we're looking for Alex. Anybody know where he's at?"

He was perfect. Friendly, but to the point. Strong, but not threatening.

Everybody turned to look at the inked older guy. The guy stood up and walked across the porch toward Mateo, his tattoos seeming to morph as he went.

That's when it hit me: he was the Loco who'd attacked the biker at the theater—the guy Mateo had pistol-whipped. Did he recognize Mateo?

"How you know our boy Santo?" Tattoo asked.

I knew from Facebook that Santo was Alex's nickname. Was it because he had a good heart? Or was it one of those ironic names because he was really a devil?

If Mateo was nervous, he showed no sign of it. He nudged his chin in my direction. "Alex is my girl's little brother. He's gotta come home now and then. He's only fifteen, see, and we don't want the cops to go looking for him."

It was a risk, mentioning the cops.

I bet Tattoo didn't want the cops to start sniffing around either. He squinted at Mateo. "Yo, do I know you?"

My heart stopped.

Please, God, no.

"Nah. This is a mug people don't forget," Mateo said with a chuckle. "It's Mateo."

"Manny," Tattoo said.

I wished Mateo hadn't used his real name. What if this guy clued in later as to who he was and tracked him down?

Manny turned around and smacked the nearest guy's arm. "Jesus, didn't you hear? Go get Santo! Tell him his *hermana's* here!"

The younger guy ran inside.

Manny's face broke into a lazy, rather charming smile. "He'll be right out, *amigo*. No worries."

Moments later, Alex appeared in the doorway. Relief whooshed through me. I wanted to run up and hug him, then wring his neck.

Alex went down the steps. "What the fuck?"

Mateo took the question. "It's no big deal, man. Let's just call it a night."

Alex ignored that, continuing to stare me down. "You're stalking me now?"

I put my hands on my hips. "Thanks to you. Let's go. We'll talk in the car."

"I ain't going with you." He crossed his arms. He reminded me of a toddler at the day care. I bet if I grabbed his arm, he'd go limp and wiggly.

"You *are* going," I said.

"Get out of here, bitch!" Alex lurched forward, but Mateo got between us, putting a hand on his chest.

"Back off, Alex." Mateo turned to me. "Go to the car, lock the doors. Wait for us." He handed me the keys.

I nodded. I was seething, but I knew that if I didn't walk away, I'd smack Alex.

In the car, two blocks down, I waited.

And waited.

What if Mateo couldn't convince him to come home?

Another worry set in. What if the Locos decided to intervene or if Manny suddenly recognized him from the theater?

The thought made me get out of the car. If Mateo got hurt trying to help Alex . . .

But I'd only walked half a block when I saw them heading my way. Mateo looked weary. Alex hung his head, refusing to look at me.

The car ride was painfully quiet.

When we got home, Alex slammed the car door and ran upstairs to his room. Mateo came in too.

In the living room, we sat down on opposite couches.

"How'd you get him to come home?" I asked.

"I told him that if he didn't come with us, we'd call the cops to take him home. He panicked. The Locos wouldn't appreciate the cops stopping by."

"Good call." I was relieved. But our win was temporary. "I know I didn't give you any choice in helping me, but thanks."

"I don't want to see anything bad happen to the kid." He leaned forward, placing his elbows on his knees and cracking his knuckles. "Even though it took everything I had not to punch him in the face when he disrespected you. The kid is angry. He lost his mom and his dad's not there for him. It's a lot of anger to undo. But it can be done.

"I'll stay the night." He picked up the remote and turned on the TV. "In case Alex tries to slip out."

"Oh. Thank you." I closed my eyes. I couldn't thank him enough. I was tempted to grab his hand or give him a hug. But I didn't trust myself to touch him. "I'll make up my dad's bed."

"It's all right, I'll take the couch. It'll be easier to hear if he tries to go anywhere."

"Right. Okay."

"Grace?"

I saw the hunger in his eyes, and I was a goner.

I didn't know who crossed the space first, who made the first move. I just knew that his kiss was searing hot and open-mouthed. I grabbed the back of his head, bringing him closer. We took a deep, shuddering breath, and then were kissing again. I heard him groan, and my whole body turned to water.

His tongue. His lips. God, they were more incredible than I remembered. *He wanted me.* I knew it in his touch, his ragged breathing. The way his hard body pressed me into the couch, crushing me. The way he whispered my name reverently against my mouth.

"It's killing me," he said.

What was killing him? Me?

He wrenched away suddenly, wiping his mouth. It had been a big, messy, out-of-control kiss. I wanted more.

"Grace . . ."

I was light-headed, as if I'd been breathing helium from a balloon. "What?"

"I'm sorry."

I smoothed my hands over my hair. "It's okay. My fault too."

"Not for the kiss." His dark eyes were pained. "For break-ing your heart. For letting you down. I'm sorry."

A rush of tears stung my eyes. I couldn't even speak. All the old anguish rose up like a tidal wave. I managed to nod, then I hurried upstairs.

NEED

AT 6:55 THE NEXT MORNING, I crept into the kitchen, hoping not to wake Mateo. But I wound up smashing into his bare chest.

I looked down, awed. Dark, curling chest hair trailed down to his hard stomach.

He hadn't had that before.

There was a moment of awkward shuffling before we got our bearings.

"I was just putting on coffee," he said, embarrassed. "Didn't think you'd be up yet."

That's when I realized he wasn't wearing any pants.

He wore nothing but navy boxer briefs. I drank in the sight of him, the long legs, trim hips, muscular torso. The shadow of stubble on his jawline. God, he looked good. His eyes flickered to mine, and his expression heated up. He turned around fast.

"Um—clothes." He went to the living room and grabbed his pants off the couch, pulling them on quickly. Then he put on last night's T-shirt, covering up all that skin. So sad.

"Thanks for staying over," I said, standing by the coffee-maker. I was glad I'd already showered, dressed, and put on some makeup—just in case he'd spotted me. I wasn't going to risk coming downstairs looking like a sack of crap.

"He didn't try to run last night," Mateo said.

"That's good."

"I wish I could stay to talk to him, but I've got an exam this morning. Can't miss it."

"You have an exam?" *Of course.* It was the end of April—exam time for most college students. And I'd made him go out on a mission to bring home Alex when he could've been studying. Or sleeping. "Are you ready for it?"

"Yeah." He shrugged. "It's not something you can study for. It's mostly based on instinct. It's for the driving part of my course. I've got some experience with fast driving."

"But you only slept a few hours." I bit my lip.

"I'm used to screwed-up sleep. Paramedics have to be able to adapt. I'll be fine."

"You'd better eat." I opened the fridge. "We've got eggs. Peanut butter. Jam."

"It's okay. I'll grab something at home. Gotta shower and shave before I go to school. Just coffee's good."

I was about to pour it for him, but he did it himself, adding cream. He sat down at the kitchen table to drink it. I stood at the counter with mine.

"Let him sleep in," he said. "Don't wake him for school."

I frowned. "He has to go back. If he doesn't, he could get in even more trouble."

Mateo shook his head. "That's the least of your problems. If he wants to sleep in and play video games all day, let him. At least for now. If you bug him about school, it could drive him off again. Trust me on this one. It's getting really dangerous out there. The Locos are into some serious shit. They're dealing in guns, drugs. And somehow they've pissed off the Destinos, which was a big mistake."

My stomach dropped. *The Destinos.* "That's the gang that went after Los Reyes?"

"Yeah. They went underground for a while, but now they're back, and they've set their sights on the Locos. The beef is major. I don't wanna see Alex get caught in the cross-fire. The Destinos are gonna crush the Locos." There was an edge to his voice. "It's just a matter of when."

"Scary." The coffee I was drinking turned my stomach to acid. I put it down. "I won't bug him about school, I promise."

"I'll be back tonight after dinner. My training shifts are

over now. You don't work Monday nights, right?"

"Right."

"Good. Hopefully we can keep Alex home. I'll work on him." He took another sip of coffee, then got up and dumped the rest in the sink. "I'd better go."

He grabbed his wallet and phone. I opened the front door for him. Before he could leave, I put a hand on his arm. "Good luck."

"Thanks." He smiled. I flashed back to the boy I used to know, and my heart did a flip.

As he drove away, I stared after him, gazing at the quiet, sun-drenched street.

I am not going to fall for him again, I told myself. It would be a mistake. Maybe even a disaster.

And yet a quiet voice in my head asked, *But what if it wasn't?*

True to his word, Mateo came over that evening. He made us grilled cheese and bacon sandwiches with tomato soup. Although Alex was hardly speaking to me, he wasn't going to pass up such an awesome dinner.

"So the scenario was that a baby was choking," Mateo said. The minute he'd mentioned his driving exam, Alex had perked up. "It's a Class A situation, which means you've got to get there as fast as possible. All bets are off—only thing you can't do is mow down a pedestrian. Other than that, sidewalks are in play. I made it through the course in three minutes, twenty seconds."

"Holy!" Alex said, midchew. "How long would most people take?"

"Twice that. I'm not trying to brag, but it's true. Plus I didn't hit the cyclist or the other cars."

I stared at him. "They had a cyclist on the course?"

"It was a cardboard cyclist, but still. Three people hit him. It's pretty much an automatic fail."

"Yikes." I sipped my soup.

"The next scenario was the scene of a horrific car crash, where a tractor trailer and a car collided on the highway. I had a partner for that one. We got there in five minutes, since Hunter was driving, not me. And we had to use the Jaws of Life to get the family out of the car—they're these hydraulic-powered shears that cut through metal."

"That's so awesome! Were they dummies or real people?" Alex asked eagerly.

"Dummies. Some of them were supposed to be still alive. Some obviously weren't." He glanced at me.

I shuddered. "I'd have been freaked out just by the re-enactment. I can't imagine going to the scene of a real crash. I'm glad you can do it."

"What about the truck driver?" Alex asked.

"We went over to try to get him out. He was calling for help."

"If this doesn't end well, my dinner's going to be ruined," I said.

"Sorry. Maybe I should finish the story later."

"No way!" Alex said.

I closed my eyes. "Fine. Tell us."

"We were trying to pry open the door when I noticed gas leaking from the cab of the truck. Which told me the engine must've been damaged during the crash. When you see that happening, the best option's to get the hell away."

"So what'd you do?" Alex said.

"I shouted to clear out and ran. But Hunter wouldn't go. He was working the door from the other side, and he'd almost gotten it open. See, he was one of the guys who'd hit the cyclist, and he didn't want to fail. He thought he could redeem himself if he got the guy out."

"But it didn't end well," I said dismally.

"No. There was a popping sound, which meant the truck exploded."

"Holy shit!" Alex clapped his hands together. "That's a sick story!"

Mateo grinned and took another bite of his grilled cheese.

I had to admit, I was impressed with Mateo, and not only due to his skills as a paramedic. His storytelling had helped cut the tension between Alex and me.

"I brought that movie I was talking about," Mateo said,

grabbing a DVD from his backpack and handing it to me. Of course, he hadn't been talking about any movie, but I knew what he was doing—trying to keep Alex home tonight. "It's from that list of the top horror movies of all time. It's Swedish, called *Let the Right One In*. They did an American version, but I heard it's not nearly as good."

"Looks freaky," I said. The picture on the DVD showed a child with blood dripping from his mouth. "Guess I won't be sleeping tonight."

"Lemme see." Alex snatched it from me. He examined the picture on the front, then read the back. "This looks cool."

"Should we watch it?" Mateo asked.

I nodded. "Why not?"

"Definitely," Alex said.

Well played, Mateo.

Once we'd cleared away the dishes, we put the movie on. It wasn't the typical horror movie—it was more creepy than bloody. I could tell Alex was riveted. Occasionally he'd ask Mateo a question, worried he'd miss a detail.

When the movie was over, we talked about it for a while, then I told them I was heading to bed. They said good night, only briefly breaking off the conversation as I left the room. I went to load up the dishwasher and clean the kitchen a bit first.

On my way upstairs, I paused for a second to see if I could catch a bit of their conversation.

". . . what you gotta do," Mateo was saying. "But if the Locos are anything like the Reyes used to be, you don't know what you're in for."

"I can't believe you were a Reyes, man," Alex said, awed. "They were the real deal."

"Yeah, and most of those guys are dead. I'm the lucky one. I'm still breathing."

"I can't believe they let you out. In the Locos, once you're in, that's it."

"Same with the Reyes," Mateo said. "Nobody told me I was gonna have to put my life on the line to make money for the gang. Our leader, El Toro, sent my buddy Franco to do some deals in cartel territory. They shot him dead."

"Shit."

"Yeah. I was damned if I was gonna end up on a slab just so Toro could afford to buy his Cristal, you know? I already went to juvie for doing a deal for him. So when Toro tried to send me into cartel territory, I said no."

"You said *no* to the leader? Shi-it!"

"Yeah. It didn't help that I had to say it in front of a group of them. I've never been so scared in my life. I knew he wouldn't tolerate it. He told them to . . . to hold me down—" Mateo broke off for a minute, as if digging out the words. "He took out a razor blade and cut my face. Then he told them to finish me off."

There was a long silence. For once, Alex had nothing to say.

"They left me by the docks. I thought I was dead. There was blackness all around and I couldn't see—my eyes had swollen shut. Nobody found me until the next morning. It was amazing I didn't bleed out."

Tears streamed down my cheeks. I wiped them away, trying not to make a sound.

"I woke up in the hospital three days later. Every part of me hurt, I can't even tell you. But the pain told me I was alive."

I sobbed silently into my hands. I wished I'd known what had happened to him. I wished I could've been there to help him through it.

"I heard they called me 'Matador' after that, because I'd stood up to the bull. I was the only one who'd done that and survived."

"You gotta admit, that's kind of cool," Alex said.

"I guess, but the whole thing was fucked-up. My own gang did that to me—the guys who were supposed to have my back. My own brother."

"Your brother was there when they did that to you?"

"Yeah."

"That's horrible."

"That's the Reyes for you. Gang before blood. What makes you think the Locos are any different?"

Alex didn't have an answer for that.

* * *

"So tell me this. How *good* is he?" Feenix asked me Friday night. With the early shows in progress there were no customers, so we chilled out with soft cinnamon pretzels. "I want details. Schematics. It's getting a little routine with Kenny and me. I need some inspiration."

I smiled. "Planning on a sex poem for next week?"

"Maybe."

"I got nothing for you. Read some erotica. Nina's got a whole pile of those books."

"I know. But Eddie's been borrowing them." She made an ick face. "I wish somebody would find that guy a girl. Anyway, what I'm interested in is what's going on between you and Mr. Sexy-Pants Security Guard. Spill it."

I tried to smile, but the truth was, I ached. Mateo and I hadn't been alone together for more than a few minutes in days. But the air between us was thick and hot. Even Alex had assumed we'd gotten together since Mateo was spending so much time at our place now. We didn't dare set him straight.

I was starting to think that my version of our history was warped. I'd always blamed Mateo for making me break up with him—for choosing the gang over me. But maybe I was wrong. Maybe I'd let *him* down when he'd needed me, and not the other way around.

After hearing Mateo's account of what the gang had done

to him, my feelings for him had shifted. Most guys who'd been through that would've chosen to hate the world. Instead, he'd gone back to school and built a future for himself. Mateo was stronger than I'd ever realized. He was freaking magnificent.

Feenix stared at me, waiting for me to give her something, anything.

"Based on my past experience with him, I'd say he's a sensualist."

Her eyes bulged. "What? Tell me more!"

"He's not the type of guy to rush things. I mean, he's really passionate by nature. But he's a take-his-time, appreciate-the-scenery type of guy."

She raised a brow. "The scenery?"

"He's into the five senses. Touch, taste, smell, sight, and sound." I was messing with her, but she was eating it up.

"Sound, huh? He talks dirty, I bet!"

"I keep telling you, we're not together," I said, finally getting serious. "He just drives me home sometimes and chills with my brother. When are you going to believe me?"

"When hell freezes over. You think anyone here believes you're not boning each other every damn night?"

"I told you, he's been hanging out with Alex. He's kind of mentoring him."

She glared at me. "Right. Because straight guys are just that nice. Sorry, Grace, but I don't buy it. Mateo looks like he wants to eat you with a spoon!"

"C'mon." But I couldn't disagree. Sometimes I glimpsed the heat in his eyes. He'd look away, as if he were in physical pain. It drove me nuts.

"You do know you're smiling, right?"

"I'm not." But my lips were pulling at my cheeks. Whatever this attraction was, we were enjoying it. Playing with it. With our eyes. With a passing touch. It was dangerous territory, like dabbling with a highly addictive drug. But I couldn't seem to stop.

I reminded myself that once Alex was back on track, Mateo wouldn't need to hang out with us anymore. The thought made my heart sink. I had to trust that Mateo wouldn't go off the radar anytime soon. He genuinely cared about Alex and wanted to see him go straight.

But did he care about me enough to stick around?

Later that night, Mateo drove me home.

I had something to say, something burning inside me. I should get it off my chest before I lost the courage.

"You said you were sorry for letting me down, back then," I said, taking a deep breath.

"I meant it."

"But you shouldn't be sorry. You were in a tough spot. I didn't understand how stuck you were. Maybe . . . I didn't want to understand." It was easier saying it while he was driving, while his eyes were on the road and not on me. "I know you were trapped. I hope you didn't hate me all this time for breaking up with you."

His lips pressed together. "Never. You did the right thing. My life got a whole lot worse before it got better. It would've been horrible to drag you through it with me." He was silent for a moment, then continued softly, "After all you went through with your mom, I didn't want that for you."

"But I dragged you through everything with me when Mom was sick. You didn't walk away."

"It's not the same thing." He braked at a light, the red glow reflecting onto his face. His expression was bleak. "I saw what your mom's sickness did to you. I would've done anything to take the sadness away. When I joined the gang, you had the choice to protect yourself, for once. And you did."

I'd thought so at the time, but was it true? "I think I knew, deep down, that you didn't really want to be in the Reyes. I was being selfish."

"Selfish? God, you take care of everyone around you—it's what you do. I *wish* you were more selfish."

Did he really see me that way? "I guess you forgot I'm blackmailing you."

"Exactly—you're doing something you'd never do just to help your brother."

"It's not just for Alex," I admitted. "It's for me, too. I love him, but I'm sick of dealing with him. If he keeps getting into trouble, I'll always be the one who will get the call. Dad's not around enough to handle him. I never told you this, but the reason I'm not in college right now is because my grades dropped when he got arrested last spring. I was so upset I couldn't study, couldn't finish my papers . . . and I lost my college acceptance. The worst part was that I felt like I'd let my mom down—like I should've found a way to stop Alex from getting into trouble."

"You seriously think it's your fault?"

"I don't know anymore. I just know I'm sick of cleaning up his messes. I want him to wake the fuck up and let me have a life. How selfish does that sound?"

He smiled, and my stomach quivered. "Just the right amount of selfish. It's time you looked out for yourself."

"Even if it means blackmailing you?"

"You know that's not why I'm doing this. I want to help you. And Alex."

"You are helping." I paused, wondering if I should admit what I'd overheard. "I was listening when you told him what they did to you."

"Yeah, I figured."

"How'd you know?"

"I heard you go up half the stairs."

"Oops."

"It's okay. I was telling you, too."

My eyes filled with tears. "I'm so sorry that happened to you." His face was in shadows, but I could see the outline of the scar—a reminder of that night that he faced every day in the mirror. "I understand why you don't write to your brother."

Tears rolled down my cheeks. I couldn't fight them anymore.

"Don't cry," he said, almost roughly, and reached over to grab my hand.

"I'm fine. I'm emotional. It's just how I am."

To my surprise, he made a right turn, pulling over in the nearest parking lot. He turned to me.

"I know it's how you are. You feel for other people. Sometimes too much. Their happiness is your happiness. Their pain is yours. That's why you're so good with those kids. You put yourself in their shoes, see through their eyes."

"How do you know?"

"Because I know you. I've always known you." His intensity took my breath away.

We used to have these moments when we got lost in each other's eyes—when we totally understood each other. It was happening now. An intense warmth spread through me.

"There's a downside," he said. "No matter how hard you try, you can't take away somebody else's pain."

I thought of him lying in that hospital bed. "I wish I could have taken away yours."

"I know."

There were no sounds in the car except our quiet breathing, and a muffled horn blast miles away.

"I know you don't want me to bring up the time you came over after we broke up," he said, "but I want to explain."

"You'd moved on. I understand."

He shook his head. "I never wanted to send you away like that. But the guys were watching. I didn't dare show any feelings for you in front of them. I was thinking of your safety. Toro was there. If he thought I felt anything for you, it would've given him ideas."

"What ideas?"

His jaw tightened. "To take you for himself. I'd seen him do it with other guys' girlfriends. And you're so damned pretty. I could tell he noticed you right away. So I acted like you were some crazy ex-girlfriend. If he thought I cared about you, he would've been interested."

It made sense now—the cold way he'd sent me away. "That's twisted."

"I know."

I wasn't letting him off the hook. "You could've called me to explain. You made me feel like a joke."

His eyes dropped. "I know. I thought about calling you.

But I told myself it was better if you hated me. Then it would be a clean break. You'd be free of me, and safe."

"I felt . . ." I didn't want to put it in words. I'd felt worthless, like he'd never really loved me.

There was a plea in his eyes. "I know it was the wrong thing to do. But what would you have done if I'd explained it to you? You'd have forgiven me. You might've taken me back. I couldn't let that happen. I didn't trust myself to stay away from you. We were both better off with you hating me."

"I wish I'd hated you. But I thought it was my fault—that I was too needy, too crazy."

"I'm so sorry," he said.

I wiped my tears with my fingers. "It's okay."

We sat there in silence. Eventually he pulled back onto the road and drove the rest of the way to my house.

I didn't know what was happening between us. But it felt like we'd arrived someplace we hadn't been to before. We'd arrived at honesty.

And at my house.

He turned off the engine. The lights were out.

"He's not home," I said, stating the obvious.

"Don't worry. I never thought he'd stop hanging out with them cold turkey. But I'm hoping I've given him stuff to think about." He checked his phone. "Look, he texted me. Said to tell you he'll be home by one. It's a good sign."

"He could've texted *me*," I grumbled, seeing no messages on my phone. But Mateo was right. Just the fact that Alex had checked in with him, and given himself a curfew, was progress.

"He's also reminding me that I'm taking him driving tomorrow afternoon," Mateo said. "He wants to learn."

"That's great. He'll be sixteen in August."

"He's hoping to buy a car."

"I wonder how he'll manage that without a job."

"He's been talking about looking for one."

"Has he? I'm afraid to hope. A job would keep him busy and off the streets." I unbuckled. "Want to hang out for a bit?"

I felt his hesitation. It seemed to be coming from a deep, heavy place.

"I shouldn't."

"Why not?"

"Because." The word was a growl. "You know why."

But I didn't know why. He was driving me crazy. I could hardly eat, sleep, breathe without thinking about him. We'd come to a place of openness and honesty, a place I'd never thought we could get to. And damn it, I wasn't ready for him to go home.

He took a breath, avoiding my eyes. "If I go in there, I'll be all over you."

I bit my lip against a groan. "So?" Wasn't that what he wanted? It was what *I* wanted.

"I don't think it would be smart."

Understanding clicked. He was tempted to fool around, but he wasn't looking to be tied down. He didn't think I could handle that. He thought I was too fragile. He still saw me as that girl who'd fallen apart on his front lawn.

I swung open the car door, the bright interior light coming on. "I'm not the pathetic girl I used to be, in case you were wondering."

I moved to get out of the car, but he put a hand on my thigh. "Don't say that. You were never, ever pathetic. I *loved* that girl."

Loved. Past tense. Of course. How could I have thought that he wanted to be with me again?

I must be delusional.

AMBULANCE

THE NEXT MORNING, I LOGGED into my online course and found out I got an A on my sociology paper. The teacher commented: *An interesting paper. Hopefully in college you'll continue this research. Well done.*

I pumped a fist. Awesome! If I stayed on track, my average would be back up where I needed it to be to get into college.

How ironic that my paper was on empathy. Mateo had said that feeling people's pain was my specialty.

Thinking back to last night, I cringed. I really thought we would take the next step. But I'd mistaken his attraction to me for more. He'd gotten over me long ago. He only wanted to resolve the past, not open it up again. The whole situation was painful and embarrassing.

Alex woke up around noon and slunked downstairs to the kitchen. I was in the living room on my laptop and said "hi" as he scrounged around for some food. He'd come in by one last night, as promised.

"Want scrambled eggs with cheese?" I asked.

"It's okay. Cereal's good."

He sat down at the kitchen table and ate. I knew I should wait a few minutes before trying to have a conversation with him. He was always grumpy in the morning. It was a family trait.

"Got an A on my paper," I said, when he'd almost finished his food.

"What paper?"

"For my online sociology course."

"Oh, that's cool. Maybe you could do some of my papers for me."

"I'd totally help you." It might not be too late for him to pass some of his courses, but I knew not to push him. Mateo was right—keeping Alex from becoming a full member of the Locos was the priority. School could wait.

"When's Mateo coming over?" I asked.

He glanced at the microwave clock. "Twelve thirty. He says he's a sick driver and he's gonna teach me all the crazy-ass techniques." Alex shoveled in the last of his cereal and got up. "I'd better shower."

Mateo showed up a few minutes later looking freshly

showered but tired. Maybe he'd slept as little as I had. His expression was closed off. The chasm between us was deep enough to fall into.

His dark eyes were uncertain. "Alex here?"

"He'll be down in a minute. Come in."

He did, hands in his pockets, back to the door. I went back to typing on the laptop.

Alex bounded down the stairs. "Hey, man, you ready?"

Mateo fist-pounded him. "The question is, are *you* ready?"

"Damn straight."

They headed out.

I ducked my head out the door. "Bring him home in one piece, okay?"

"Promise," Mateo said, and they got in the car.

Mateo wasn't at work that night.

I kept glancing toward the glass doors. It was odd. He hadn't missed a shift since he'd started working here, and he hadn't seemed sick earlier today. Alex had come home two hours later, pumped. They'd had an awesome time driving, then Mateo had taken him out to eat.

By seven, I texted Mateo: Where are you?

No reply. That was odd too. Now that his exams were done, he was waiting for his certification to come through before he could take paid shifts as a paramedic. So where was he?

"What's with the mood today?" Feenix asked, way too perceptive.

"Nothing. Mateo took Alex driving today. They had a great time."

"What about you and Mateo?"

Screw pride—I might as well tell her. "He blew me off."

Her eyes bugged out. "In the good way or the bad way?"

"Bad way."

"You're a liar!"

"I'm serious. I invited him in last night. My brother wasn't home. And he said no."

"He said no!" she screamed, startling a customer who'd been approaching us. The customer made a *WTF?* face and headed for popcorn instead.

"Mateo said that if he came in, he'd want to . . . you know. But then he didn't come in."

Her jaw dropped. "That makes no sense. Has he got another girl?"

"I don't know." That possibility had occurred to me, but I hadn't wanted to think about it. I knew that when I'd texted him sometimes, even late at night, he wasn't at home. He never said where he was or what he was doing. Was he with a girl? He was often texting friends—was one of them a girlfriend?

"He might have someone," I said. "Sometimes he's out really late, and I don't know what he's up to."

"He could be on one of those hook-up apps. Maybe he calls himself *Scarred Sensualist*. With a bod like that, he could be getting hundreds of right swipes a day."

"Is that supposed to be comforting?"

"No, I guess not." She put an arm around me. "Sorry."

"It's okay. He might have a girlfriend, but I don't think he's the casual hook-up type." I sighed. "You're lucky that you've got Kenny. You guys are freaking beautiful together."

She smiled. "Best man I ever met."

"I was worried when you said things were getting a bit routine."

"Don't be. He's my forever boo, my sweet Kenny Bear. I won't go screwing it up."

"Better not."

Luke's swanky crib.

Throbbing music.

My gaze swept the room. There were twice as many people as usual and lots of cute guys.

I checked my phone just in case Mateo had gotten back to me. He hadn't. He usually texted me back, but I guess last night had changed things. He was pulling away. Must be history repeating itself.

Whatever. It was time to party.

I drank. Danced. Although I kept thinking about Mateo, I partied like it didn't matter.

I was two drinks and two Jell-O shots in by the time I slammed on the brakes. I was pretty buzzed, maybe borderline drunk. I made sure to secure a ride with Feenix so she and Kenny didn't take off without me.

Luke had his eyes on me tonight. I couldn't ignore that fact.

At some point we were dancing together.

His hand was on my hip, and he held a red fruity drink in the other. For such a large guy, he moved well. Sensual, fluid. I was getting heated up.

The truth was, I was *already* heated up. Ever since Mateo had come back into my life, I'd been in overdrive. I was a lit cigarette, and Luke wanted to take a drag. I was tempted to let him.

"I like you," he said, his breath hot in my ear.

I didn't know what to say. I just smiled and kept dancing.

Playing with fire.

He steered my hips closer, and then we were grinding. I saw his eyes go hooded as he watched our pelvises grind together.

I had to admit, in the deepest, darkest part of myself, I was taking satisfaction in these moments. Maybe Luke saw something Mateo didn't.

"We need to talk," Luke said close to my ear, his breath rippling down my neck. His hazel eyes were suddenly serious. "Meet me near the bathroom in five minutes. Don't make it obvious."

That was strange, but I went along with it.

Five minutes later, I stood in the sleek, hardwood hallway outside the bathroom. Luke walked up to me, grabbed my hand, and pulled me across the hall into his bedroom.

Closing the door, he said, "Sorry about that. I wanted to talk to you alone and didn't want to start any rumors."

"About what?"

"This." He cupped my face in his hands and kissed me.

The game was over, I realized. The flirtation, the fun, it was over. This was real. I had to choose, and I had to choose now.

I kissed him back, opening my mouth. His kiss was hungry. My body burned, and I wanted more.

He's not the one you want.

I tried to shut the voice out. He pressed me into the wall, his body molding against mine.

A bunch of things went through my head. I knew I wasn't going to sleep with him. I could continue to enjoy this, suspended in this sexy haze, or I could take a step back.

In a minute, I told myself. I'd take a step back in one more minute.

When I pulled away, he groaned, and took a second to

compose himself before looking up. "Aw fuck," he said, but he was smiling lazily.

I smiled back at him. "It's fun, but . . ."

"It's okay. I understand."

A sudden sadness came over me. It was never Luke's arms I'd wanted around me, never his kiss I'd wanted to taste. He'd been a temporary distraction to fill the void left by Mateo.

Luke tipped up my chin. "Everything okay?"

"Yeah. I'd better go."

"All right." His eyes glittered with disappointment. "I'll be out in a few minutes."

I slipped out and went back to the living room, where the party was in full force. I checked my phone.

Ten missed calls from Mateo. Three texts.

Get to Mercy Hospital right away. Alex is hurt.

Feenix and Kenny dropped me off at the hospital. I ran inside the automatic doors while they went to park the car. Mateo was there waiting for me.

"Is he okay? What happened?" I looked around, ready to run in any direction.

"There was a fight. He went down on his head. Blacked out. But he was awake a few minutes ago, talking. I think he'll be okay."

"Thank God." Only then did I realize that there was a guy standing beside us. He had striking blue eyes and a stone serious face. Ignoring me, he walked away.

"Who was that?"

"A friend. It doesn't matter."

Feenix and Kenny hurried in. She grabbed my arm. "How is he?"

"Okay, I think," I said.

"Let's go see him," Mateo said.

Feenix held on to my arm as we followed Mateo. He took us to the elevator, where he pressed the button for the third floor. He led us down another hallway before stopping in front of a room.

He opened the door, and we peered in. Alex lay in a bed, eyes closed. He looked way too still. I watched him for a few seconds until I saw his chest move with a breath.

I turned to Mateo, panic rising. "I thought you said he was talking."

"He was when they took him for X-rays. They must've given him pain meds for his head—that would put him to sleep right away. Let's talk to the nurse."

We went up to the nurse's station. "Excuse me!" Feenix said loudly, causing the nurse to look up immediately. "We need to talk to somebody about Alex Dillane. This is his sister."

"Just a minute, I'll find someone for you," the nurse said.

A couple of minutes later, a nurse in turquoise scrubs approached us, carrying a chart. "Hi. I'm Candace. Alex took a knock to the head, but we did some X-rays and didn't see any significant brain swelling. Dr. Weller said we should keep him overnight for observation, but we expect to discharge him in the morning."

I'd been holding my breath for the last few minutes. Now I was able to let it out. "Thanks."

"If you'd come over to the desk, there are some papers we need you to fill out. Insurance information and such."

My relief was replaced with a new dread. "Okay." I didn't want to think about how much this hospital stay would cost.

She looked at the others. "Since it's well past visiting hours, I'm afraid you'll have to leave," she said, then headed to the nursing station.

Feenix gave me a hug. "You stay strong. He'll be fine."

"Thanks. I'll call you tomorrow."

"Take care, Grace," Kenny said.

"I will."

Mateo whispered in my ear, "I'll meet you in his room."

The three of them headed down the hall, disappearing around a corner. I went to the nurse's station and filled out the forms. Alex was covered by Dad's plan, but it wouldn't cover everything. I flashed back to Mom's medical bills. They'd kept coming for a year after she died. Her illness had taken every penny we had.

I went back to the room. Mateo was sitting by the bed. I was glad that he hadn't left. I needed to find out what the hell was going on.

"What happened to him?"

He raked his hands through his hair. "The Destinos went after the Locos tonight. I got a tip that it was going to happen. Showed up just as it was going down. Alex got knocked out, but I managed to get him out of there. The whole thing was a mess . . . a lot of people got hurt. Don't know if anybody got killed."

I nodded, digesting all of this. Mateo had rushed to the scene to help Alex, while I'd been partying and making out with Luke.

I felt sick inside.

"How did you know where he was?"

"I have friends on the street who keep me informed."

"Like that guy I just saw?"

"Yeah, like that guy." He bent his head and put his hands on his knees. He looked beyond exhausted. He looked wrecked.

On instinct, I put my arms around him, laying my head on his back. Tears were locked inside me. "Thank you."

I squeezed him, and he reached up and grasped my hand. "Grace." It came out like a sigh.

We stayed that way for a long time.

When we pulled apart, I said, "Go home and sleep. We'll talk tomorrow."

"I'll give you a ride."

I shook my head. "I'll stay with him. I want to be here when he wakes up."

He nodded. "Text me in the morning."

"I will."

We both stood. I gave him another hug. I wanted to wrap not just my arms, but my soul, around him. "Good night, Mateo."

EXPOSED

I WOKE UP ON A fold-out chair with kinks all over and an aching heart. Around four a.m., a car crash victim had been wheeled into the room. I'd hardly slept since then. I kept picturing Alex getting hurt in the fight and Mateo swooping in to rescue him.

And me kissing Luke.

When Alex woke up, he saw me and rolled his eyes. "Do I get a lecture?" he grumbled.

"Do you need one?"

"No."

"I'm pretty good at keeping my mouth shut these days, don't you think?"

"Yeah. My head hurts."

"You have a concussion."

"Duh. I guess Mateo called you."

I nodded.

"What did he tell you?"

Alex wanted to hear Mateo's version before telling his.

"He didn't tell me much—just that there was a fight and you got knocked out."

"Yeah." Alex glanced toward the window. There was stuff he didn't want to say. No surprise there. I *would* get the whole story, but now wasn't the time to demand details.

"Just tell me one thing for now."

He looked at me from below droopy lids.

"Are you going back to the Locos?"

"No," he said fiercely. "They almost got me killed. If Mateo hadn't been there, I'd have been . . . fucked."

I believed him. Whatever had gone down last night had changed his view of the Locos. Maybe *this* was what he needed to wake him up.

"Alex?" A gravelly voice called from the doorway.

Dad hurried into the room. He bent over the bed. "Grace said you were hurt."

Alex's lower lip jutted. I didn't know if he wanted to give attitude or cry. "Hey, Dad," he said, and reached out for a hug.

Dad drove us home in his girlfriend's Ford Taurus—he'd borrowed it to get here as soon as possible. Maybe I should feel bad for making that panicked call on the way to the hospital and telling him to come home right away. Alex wasn't exactly at death's door.

But I wasn't sorry. Dad needed to be here.

Alex slept the day away. The doctor had told me to wake him every two hours to make sure he was okay. I'd ask him a couple of questions, like what his name was and how old he was. He'd curse under his breath, answer the dumb questions, and wave me away.

Dad went to bed too. He'd driven nine hours straight without stopping.

I spent the day pacing the house and making chili, since I didn't know what else to do.

Around five p.m., Dad woke up and shuffled downstairs, saying that the smell of the chili had woken him. I served him a bowl along with some buttered bread.

Dad looked better than usual these days. I could tell his girlfriend, Carol Ann, had been making him over. The clothes were new: a soft plaid shirt and jeans that actually fit him. His sandy-colored hair was cut neatly, and his brows, ear, and nose hair had all been trimmed. Instead of the usual stubble, he was clean-shaven. He looked ten years younger.

After shoveling in a few bites and drinking some water, he asked, "What happened to him last night?"

"He was hanging around with a gang, and they got into a fight with a rival gang. He promised me he's not going back to them."

Dad nodded, having another spoonful of chili. "What gang was he in?"

"They're called the Locos."

"Stupid name." He tore his bread in half. "Is he going to school?"

"He's been going this past week, but before that, he was skipping a lot."

"I'll talk to him."

"You have to be careful," I said. "He's sensitive right now. Just don't set him off. Let him recover first."

"Don't worry."

I almost laughed. I shouldn't worry?

"Somebody has to."

He kept eating as if I hadn't said it. Dad had selective hearing. He didn't like confrontation.

"How long are you staying?" I asked, ready for the worst. Now that he knew Alex was going to be okay, would he leave tonight?

"I'll stay the week."

"The week?" I couldn't hide my surprise.

He nodded. "I told Steve I couldn't do the second load,

family emergency. I'll regrout the bathroom. Tiles coming loose. Do a few other things."

You're here to fix the house? Dad never sat still when he was home. He was always "tinkering" as Mom used to call it. Always something to fix, something to do. I had no idea how he made his living as a long-haul trucker when the guy couldn't sit still at home.

"I'm glad you're staying."

His gaze flickered up, as if to check if I meant it, then he went back to eating.

The upside of Alex's head injury was that he had no fight left. For the next few days, his world was his bed, the kitchen, and the living-room couch. He moved around heavily, like he was dragging the weight of the world with him.

His phone was off, sitting on his dresser. It didn't move. He hadn't once used the computer.

He was cutting the gang off. That must be it.

I called Yolanda to let her know I wouldn't be coming in this week. I explained what happened to Alex and told her that I wanted to keep an eye on him and spend some time with Dad. She was totally supportive.

"One more thing," I said. "Maybe you could take Sofia aside and tell her I'll miss her."

"Of course."

My heart felt heavy. I hoped Sofia wouldn't feel abandoned.

This was what Mateo had been talking about, I realized—the empathy, which was both a good and bad thing. I wondered if he ever had the same problem. As a paramedic in training, he'd probably seen some awful things, and would see even more on the job. How did he deal with it? He must have a way, or he wouldn't have chosen that career.

Thursday night, I went back to work at the theater. It was good knowing Dad was at home. I knew Alex was feeling down, and I didn't want him to be alone.

When I got to work, I was hoping to dodge Luke. If he had any sense, he'd avoid me for a while. It would undoubtedly be superawkward. Unfortunately, the second he saw me at the booth, he said he wanted to talk in his office.

Shit.

I walked in, my hands twisting together. "Hey."

"Hey, Grace." He was sitting behind his desk, his arms folded across his chest. I couldn't help flashing back to Saturday night when he'd kissed me. What had I been thinking?

I wished I could put it down to the alcohol, but it wouldn't be true. I'd been feeling self-destructive. I'd been horny as hell and wanted to punish Mateo.

"Is your brother doing okay?"

I let out a breath, relieved. He just wanted to know about Alex. "He's all right. Still dizzy at times, but getting better."

"You ran off in a hurry Saturday night. We were all worried about you."

"It was scary."

Luke tapped his chin thoughtfully. "I hate to ask this, but is your brother in a gang?"

"He was planning on joining the Locos, but he's changed his mind. I don't know what happened but . . . it looks like he's done with them."

Luke nodded. "I hope you're right. When I was his age, God, I was in the thick of it. Fights, drug dealing, all the shit you can imagine. It took me a long time to claw my way out." His mouth twisted. "My best friend and I were doing a major deal one night. We had a hundred Gs worth of dope on us. Then the cops showed up. I got away. He didn't."

"What happened to your friend?"

"He got fifteen years."

"That's awful."

"Yeah. I was just as guilty as him, but he never gave me up." He stared off for a minute, then blinked back into the moment. "Anyway, good thing your brother has you looking out for him."

"Thanks. My dad's in town, so that helps."

"Good to hear."

I was about to make my exit when he said my name. *Uh-oh.* I turned around.

He cleared his throat. "Things got a bit, um, out of hand Saturday night, don't you think?"

I could feel my cheeks burning. I nodded.

"I probably shouldn't have, um, made that move. I thought . . ." Luke was actually blushing. "I just want to say it won't happen again. I'm sorry."

It was nice of Luke to take the blame, but we'd both messed up. "There's no need to be sorry. It was both of us. But yeah, it's definitely not a good idea. So, uh, thank you."

He nodded, and I booked it out of his office. I went to the bathroom to let the color drain from my cheeks. That was so awkward. At the same time, kudos to Luke for owning it and apologizing. I respected that.

Back at the booth, Feenix and I sold a few pretzels, chatting in between customers. She'd texted me every day asking for updates on Alex and on how I was holding up. She'd been there for me when I needed her, 100 percent.

"Tell me if I'm out of line, but I've been dying to ask you," Feenix whispered. "Did you and Luke hook up?"

My face turned red. Oh my God, was that a rumor going around? Did everyone think I'd just gone into his office for an illicit kiss?

"Why would you think that?"

"Kenny said he saw you duck out of Luke's bedroom."

Seriously? Did I need this? No.

"Did he tell anyone?"

"Only me. So it's true?"

"We kissed. It was a mistake. That's all."

She nodded. "Good choice."

"I know. He's my freaking boss."

"Yeah, definitely not a good power dynamic. But the main problem's that he's in love with himself. He can't pass anything with a reflection without checking himself out. Anyone who gets with Luke won't just be competing against other girls— they'll be competing with his ego."

"You called it," I said.

"I don't mean to hurt your feelings, but even though he started the night with you, he ended it with someone else."

"Oh yeah?" I felt no disappointment. Nothing except a faint amusement. "Did he? Anybody I know?"

"One of the girls who works at Caliente's."

"Well, I'm glad he had a better night than I did."

Mateo had been right about Luke. He was bad news for a girl who wanted something more. Something real.

A girl like me.

Scanning the theater for Mateo, I spotted him near the glass doors. I remembered putting my arms around him in the hospital room. How could I ever repay him for helping Alex? I didn't want to think of what might've happened if he hadn't been there.

Mateo came up later for a pretzel, the moment Feenix went on break.

"How's it going?" he asked.

"Good. Tonight's pretzel is on me. It's the least I can do, considering what you did for Alex. I'll give you the freshest, fluffiest one."

When he smiled, a knot formed in my stomach. I had the sudden urge to confess that I'd made out with Luke, but that it hadn't meant anything.

I should never have thought Mateo didn't care. He cared enough to put his life on the line for Alex, didn't he? Even though he was gun-shy about having a relationship with me, I should never have written him off.

I didn't tell him that, though. I just handed him the pretzel and a Sprite, using my own money in the cash register.

"Thanks." He took a bite of the pretzel, chewed for a few seconds. "I'll drive you home later."

"You don't have to."

His eyes didn't leave mine. "I want to."

"Okay, sure. My dad's still in town . . ."

"I don't have to come in."

"All right. Well, thanks."

I was oddly nervous for the rest of the night. With Alex recovering and staying away from the Locos, did Mateo have any reason to hang out with us anymore? Once Dad left, would

Mateo start coming over again?

In the car an hour later, Mateo said, "So Alex is doing all right?"

"I think so. I mean, he seems a little depressed. But he hasn't been using his phone or the computer, so he can't be contacting any of the Locos. He's been totally unplugged."

"Good."

"He's being really vague about what happened that night. I'm hoping you can fill in the blanks for me. He said he doesn't want to have anything to do with the Locos anymore. I want to know why."

"Sometimes it's best not to know the details."

I stared at him. "Are you serious? I have to know. What's to say he won't change his mind tomorrow?"

"He won't."

"Then why don't *you* tell me what happened? You said you helped him get away from the Destinos. So why does he now hate the Locos, too?"

"The Locos didn't give him the backup he was hoping for."

Oh. Was that it? When the Destinos pounced, his guys didn't back him up? It made sense. Still, I sensed there was more to it than that.

He pulled into the driveway.

"You should come in," I said, "if it doesn't bother you that my dad's home."

"I can't. I've gotta be somewhere. I'll stop by Saturday night unless you're going to Luke's after work."

"I'm not. I just want to hang out with Alex."

"Then we'll hang out together."

Butterflies fluttered in my stomach. "Cool."

Reluctantly, I went inside. Dad and Alex were on the couch watching one of the *Expendables* movies. Gyro wrappings and empty chip bags were on the coffee table. It was good to see them chilling together.

"Who dropped you off?" Dad asked.

"My friend Mateo."

"Her *boyfriend* Mateo," Alex said.

Dad frowned. "Is he the same Mateo from years ago?"

"Yeah, same one. He's getting his paramedic certification."

Dad looked impressed. "Really? They do well, paramedics."

"He's teaching me to drive," Alex said. He was lying on the couch with his feet propped up. "I'm gonna take the test on my birthday or as soon after as I can. Now all I need is a car."

"We can talk about that," Dad said.

Was he joking? Dad didn't even have a car himself. He used the cab of his truck whenever he needed to do errands.

"I've been thinking about getting Grace a car," Dad said.

That was news to me. I'd asked for one many times—just a cheap one that would get me from A to B. But he'd said he didn't have the money. Things were different now, I guess. He might've saved up some money after all.

Dad scratched his chin. "Maybe you two could share it. How about this, Alex? You get yourself a part-time job so you can pay for your insurance, and we'll go look at something the week of your birthday."

"Sure, I was planning to get a job anyway," Alex said. "Can I choose the car?"

"No way. I pay, I choose. Carol Ann's Taurus is ten years old but still drives really good. I'm thinking something like that. Sound fair?"

We both nodded. I was glad Alex knew better than to push it.

"Great. You'll need a car to drive up to Atlanta to see Carol Ann and me anyway. She keeps saying she wants to meet you two."

Alex and I looked at each other. If that was true, I wished Dad had made it happen already. They'd been dating for at least six months now.

"We don't know much about her," I said carefully. "She's a teacher, right?"

Dad nodded. He probably thought he'd told me that, but he hadn't. Out of curiosity, I'd looked her up on Facebook, though I hadn't sent her a friend request. She was an elementary school teacher in Brookhaven, Atlanta, and often posted scrapbooking tips and recipes from Pinterest. She seemed normal enough. I was relieved that she wasn't some stripper who was after what little money Dad had.

"Does she have any kids?" Alex asked. I'd been wondering about that too.

"No, she's never been married. She's real nice, you'll see. Directs the kids' choir at her church. And she can cook. Boy, can she cook. You'll like her."

That remained to be seen.

Dad left for Atlanta Saturday morning. Alex got up to say good-bye, then went back to bed. I gave Dad a hug, and he promised to come back in a couple of weeks. He also left an envelope of cash, which would come in handy.

I spent most of the day finishing up my final assignment for sociology. If I didn't screw it up, I should get an A in the course. Which meant my marks should be high enough to get into ECE—again.

I made pasta with meatballs for dinner. Alex and I ate at the kitchen table. We'd been eating dinner together since Dad got here, and I hoped we'd continue.

"Mateo's coming over after work tonight," I said, forking some pasta. "Maybe we could watch another horror movie."

"Sure." But Alex didn't seem that excited. He took a few bites. "I'd be locked up right now if it weren't for him. He tell you that?"

"He said he helped get you away from the scene. That's all he said."

"Yeah, well. There's a lot he hasn't said."

"What do you mean?"

He rubbed a hand over his face. "I mean the reason he was there in the first place."

I put my fork down. He had my attention.

"I shouldn't have gone there that night. It was my own fucking fault. But the Locos were meeting a shipment, and Animale said they needed the man power."

I gritted my teeth. Animale. Such a good friend. "Shipment of what?"

"He wouldn't tell me. But I eventually found out it was guns. We had to unload a truck full of boxes. Biggest mistake of my life. When the Destinos jumped us, shit went crazy. Next thing I knew, I was on the ground. When I tried to get up, a Destino kicked me down. Mateo told him to let me go."

"And he listened to Mateo?" I didn't understand. Did Mateo have a weapon? "Why?"

He diverted his eyes. "Animale started shooting, the stupid son of a bitch. Didn't want to give up the shipment to the Destinos. Didn't want to give up his cut. He grabbed Mateo from behind and shoved the gun into his ribs."

I put a hand over my mouth. "Oh God."

"Mateo got lucky. His friend grabbed Animale by the neck

and yanked him away. Animale pulled the trigger at the same time—it's amazing Mateo didn't get shot."

My heart was pounding now. I'd had no idea that Mateo had almost gotten shot while trying to help Alex. Why didn't he tell me? "Thank God Mateo brought his friend with him."

"Trust me, *all* his friends were with him." Alex met my eyes, and he looked almost regretful. "I take it you don't know about him."

"Don't know what?"

He sighed. "I figured he wouldn't want you to know. He's gonna kill me if I tell you. I probably shouldn't. I mean, I owe him. But still, you're my sister. I gotta look out for you."

"For God's sake, what are you trying to tell me?"

"He's a Destino."

TWISTED

MY WORLD SPUN. *"WHAT?"*

"Yeah, I was pretty freaked myself. He's been lying this whole time—letting me spill my guts about the Locos when he's one of their enemies. It's fucked-up. If Animale hadn't pulled up his mask, I still wouldn't know he was a Destino."

"Wait a minute—he was wearing a *mask*? Are you sure it was even Mateo?"

"A hundred percent sure. And yeah, the Destinos wear ski masks. That's their MO. They wear them because they don't want people to know who they really are."

I had no words. No coherent thoughts. "He . . . he told me he wasn't in a gang."

"He lied."

But had he lied to me? Had Mateo said he wasn't in a gang or just that he wasn't in Los Reyes?

"The guy's slick," Alex said. "I don't know why he started hanging out with me in the first place. I guess because he was into you. The Destinos hate the Locos."

I was the one who'd asked Mateo to hang out with Alex. I'd forced him to, not knowing he was in a rival gang. Why didn't he just tell me he was a Destino? I would've let him off the hook with Alex. I wouldn't have ratted him out to Luke.

Mateo had seemed so genuine about having turned his life around. How could he have forgotten his experiences with the Reyes and joined another gang?

Or was everything he'd said since he came back into my life bullshit?

My stomach felt sick. I pushed my plate away.

Alex was watching me, regret on his face. "I've been debating all week whether to tell you or keep my mouth shut. But even though Mateo helped me out that night, somebody needs to look out for you. You don't want to be with him if he's a Destino. They're a bunch of psychos. Everybody's scared of them."

Somehow I'd thought Mateo and I would end up together. Deep down, I'd even convinced myself that helping out my brother was an act of love . . . for me. But if Mateo was in the Destinos, we were over before we'd begun.

I pictured my arms around him in the hospital room, pictured him grabbing my hand. I'd never felt as connected to him as in that moment.

I remembered the night he'd refused to come into my house. I knew he'd wanted me, physically anyway, but he'd held himself back. I understood now. He knew I'd never agree to be with a Destino and that I'd feel betrayed if I ever found out.

"Are you okay?" Alex asked.

I almost laughed. I couldn't remember the last time Alex cared about how I was feeling. Had the head injury knocked some feeling into him? "I don't know if I'm okay, to be honest. I guess . . . it's over with me and Mateo." There was no use in explaining to Alex that we weren't actually together since we'd let him believe that we were.

"I'm sorry, Grace. I thought you should know."

"Of course. You did the right thing."

I wondered if I should tell Alex that I'd blackmailed Mateo into hanging out with him. But I didn't want him to think that Mateo hadn't cared about him. Obviously he had, or he wouldn't have stepped in when another Destino was beating him up.

"I feel like shit about this, but you're better off," Alex said.

I nodded. Logically, I was better off. But I wanted to run to the bathroom and cry.

"I promise, I'm done with the Locos. I see who they are

now—especially Animale." He shuddered. "You saw through him right away, but I wouldn't listen. I'm sorry I was such an asshole to you."

His words undid me. In a million years I would never have expected an apology from him. Was the old Alex back? That loving kid who'd been crushed by Mom's death?

I burst into tears.

My dream was coming true. Alex was really turning around.

But Mateo was gone.

Again.

I ran to the bathroom and shut the door, running the tap to muffle my sobs. Why did it have to hurt so much? Why was losing him now just as painful as when I'd lost him back then?

I was supposed to see Mateo tonight at work. He was planning to come over later. I couldn't handle it. I took out my phone and texted Luke. I'm sorry I've missed so much work, but I don't feel well tonight. I can't come in. Sorry again.

One night when I wouldn't have to see Mateo. But what about tomorrow?

The doorbell rang around ten.

Alex cursed and paused his video game. We both knew who it was. I got up, checked the peephole, and opened the door.

Mateo took in my face. "Everything okay? Luke said you called in sick."

"I'm not sick."

He moved as if to come in, but I didn't step out of the way. He frowned. "Your dad still here?"

"Left this morning."

He saw the coldness on my face. "What is it then?"

"I heard you're a Destino."

"*What?*" He took this in, then shouldered past me and stalked toward Alex. "You little shit."

"I had to tell her," Alex insisted. "She has a right to know."

Mateo looked like he was about to whop his ass. "You don't know anything about the Destinos. I would've explained everything to you if you'd given me the chance. You haven't been answering calls all week."

I got between them. "Doesn't sound like there's anything to explain. You can do what you want, Mateo. It's your life."

"There's a lot to explain," he said between gritted teeth.

"I appreciate you helping me out," Alex said. "I'm sorry Animale tried to shoot you. Yeah, it's fucked-up. But you never told me you were a Destino. The whole time I was talking about the Locos, I had no idea who I was really talking to."

Mateo's lips tightened. "So you think I was spying on you, delivering information to the Destinos? Sorry to break it to you, but you didn't know shit about what the Locos were doing. You didn't even know it was a gun shipment until you got there. Am I right?"

Alex's face reddened.

"I texted you and tried to get you not to go. Don't you remember?"

Alex hung his head, not saying anything.

"Your boy Animale shot at me and my friends. Lucky he can't shoot for shit." He stood in front of Alex, who refused to look at him. "If I'd left you there, you know what would've happened? You'd have been arrested. With all the guns and coke in that truck—yeah, there was coke, too—you'd have gotten locked up. You think anybody would care that you're fifteen? With charges like that, you'd have done time in juvie, then moved to adult. You'd be rotting away in prison just like my brother. Didn't I show you his letters about his sorry-ass life? I saved you from that. And you repay me by talking shit about me to Grace."

Alex's eyes welled up, and he put his hands over his face.

"Leave him alone!" I grabbed Mateo's arm, trying to pull him away from my brother, but he wouldn't budge. "You've made your point, okay? Just go."

His head whipped my way, eyes flashing. "I'm not going anywhere. Not until you hear me out."

The intensity in his eyes made me take a step back. "Fine." I turned to Alex. "Go upstairs. We're going to talk."

Alex ran upstairs.

"It's your life, Mateo." I wrung my hands. "It's my fault, this situation. I'm the one who made you help Alex. But if you'd just told me you were a Destino, I would've let you off the hook."

He looked at me steadily. "The Destinos are an underground gang. We're not like the Locos, who go around bragging. Nobody knows who we are. I couldn't tell you. Besides . . ." He took a breath. "I knew I could help Alex after that first night. I wanted to try. I felt bad about walking out of his life, you know. I wanted to make it right."

I nodded, blinking back tears. "I know."

"The Destinos aren't some street gang full of criminals. We do good out there. You can't compare us to the Locos."

"Can't I? So you don't use violence to get what you want? Because I hear the Destinos are pretty talented at kicking the shit out of anyone who messes with them. Wasn't it one of *your* guys who knocked Alex out?"

His nostrils flared. "Don't blame my guy for what happened. We were stopping a shipment of guns and drugs that would've made its way to the streets. Alex should never have been there in the first place. It's on him. He's no victim." He was standing in front of me now, gripping my shoulders. "Why are you crying?"

"Because . . . you're a Destino."

I saw the raw emotion on his face. "And you don't want me anymore, now that you know," he said quietly.

My heart was dying in my chest. "You're killing me, Mateo. Don't you know that?"

"I know how it feels."

He hugged me, squeezing me tight. His arms felt as right and perfect as they always had. I loved him—in spite of everything.

I sobbed. "You know I can't do this."

He pulled back, searching my eyes. "Can't you?"

"Of course not! I can't be with someone in a gang! I want a better life than that. I've spent the last year worrying about Alex. Every night I worried that he'd get arrested or end up dead in a ditch somewhere. I can't do the same with you. I can't. Didn't you tell me I should protect myself?"

"I did." He took a breath. I expected him to argue. I wanted him to. "You're right."

I looked at him. So that was it then?

"Please keep my secret," he said softly.

"I will, but . . ." My words trailed off. *Please don't go. I can't lose you again.*

His lips brushed my forehead, a last good-bye.

Then he moved away, as my heart shattered into a million pieces.

* * *

Two nights later, I stood in front of a packed house at Oz Kafé. I scanned the crowd. They were artsy types, cradling specialty coffees, organic teas, and flutes of beer. Nerves coursed through me, but they felt good. It was nice to feel something other than grief over Mateo.

I cleared my throat before stepping up to the mike.

Shut your eyes
Shut your mouth
Shut off the voice
Spinning in your head
Shut the blinds
Shut me out
Find another girl instead.

Shut me down
Shut me off
Snuff me out like a candle flame
Shut the door
Shut your heart
Give me something, just once, instead of pain.

Drive a nail through my hand
And a stake through my heart

Drive yourself, and me, crazy
You have it down to an art.

Take down your walls
Cut off your pride
You always promised
This crazy life
Is a misery ride.

You were right.

By Saturday night, Feenix had had enough. "I wish Mateo would quit," she said. "Isn't he a paramedic yet? Can't he go save some lives?"

Although Feenix didn't know the details, she knew something serious went down between Mateo and me last weekend. My poem was a dead giveaway, not to mention the fact that we avoided each other like a nasty stomach flu. I was determined not to spiral down a well of sadness like I had when we broke up four years ago. But there was a hole in my chest now. I just couldn't accept that he belonged to another gang after what the Reyes had put him through. It made no sense.

"Are you gonna tell me what he did to you?" Feenix asked. "That poem of yours was harsh—though undeniably awesome. You guys don't even talk." She shuddered. "It's damn uncomfortable."

"He didn't do anything bad. We just decided it wasn't going to work. Well, *I* decided."

"Ah, I get it," she said, nodding. "And now he thinks you're a snob for writing him off?"

"I don't know. But you're right—it would be nice if he quit this job. I was here first."

Mateo had said he needed this job. I doubted he'd quit before he started getting paid as a paramedic. Cold turkey would be better than having to avoid him at work. I knew I'd hurt him. But did he have any clue how much he'd hurt me?

I'd lost him to a gang.

Twice.

I'd wanted him to be the hero who could help Alex, but I hadn't bothered to find out who he really was. My idea that Mateo had reformed had been a fantasy. He'd never put his past behind him. He might've been forced to join Los Reyes all those years ago, but he was obviously in the Destinos by choice.

I'd gotten what I wanted, though. Alex had finally turned around. He'd cut off the gang completely. He'd even gone back to school this week without any nagging from me. My prayer had been answered. Losing Mateo was the price.

But why did there always have to be a price?

The one thing he'd asked was that I keep his secret. Being a Destino meant any number of people would want him dead. How could he want that for himself, especially when his brother was spending his life in prison?

"Whaddaya say we go to Luke's tonight?" Feenix said. "You need to party out the pain."

"I would, but I want to be home with Alex. He's pretty lonely."

Alex had gone from being with the gang daily to being on his own. He wouldn't be getting back with his pregang friends—not after what he'd done to Leon. Alex confessed to me that he was nervous about going out at all. He was worried about running into Animale.

"You could bring him to Luke's if you want," Feenix said. "Kenny could swing by and pick him up."

"Some time, maybe. I don't think he's up for it yet."

Neither was I. No amount of partying could kill the pain of losing Mateo.

"Wanna watch another one?" Alex asked several hours later.

The clock on the TV said: 12:34 a.m. We'd just seen two episodes of *Game of Thrones*, and I was so tired I wasn't sure whose head had been chopped off in the last episode.

Alex was wide awake. He was used to staying up late and wasn't trying to break the cycle. On weekdays he stayed up half the night, went to school, came home and slept for two hours, then he'd do it all over again.

"I'm zonked."

"Aw c'mon. It's not that late. Just one more?"

"All right. One more." I was stretched out on the couch, and I figured if I drifted off during the show, he'd hardly notice.

At least Alex had found a show that he was into. He was obviously in a funk, and the fact that he still got headaches from the head injury didn't help. Anything that lifted his mood was a good thing.

Looking over at him, my heart filled up. He still had the baby pudge that made me want to pinch his cheek. I was so happy that he was home and safe—I'd stay up all night with him if I had to. I knew that Mom, wherever she was, would be relieved that he'd gotten away from the gang.

Although I fought to stay awake as the new episode started, my eyelids felt heavy.

A pounding at the door made me burst awake. Thank God we had a deadbolt, or the door would've flown off the hinges.

Fear on Alex's face. "Don't answer it!" he mouthed, putting a finger over his lips.

The Locos.

I grabbed my phone and turned it on. We didn't have a

landline, and my cell was taking way too long to power up. I had to call 911.

More pounding at the door. Alex grabbed my arm and dragged me behind the couch. "Don't get near the door. They could shoot through it."

Finally my phone powered up. I was about to dial 911 when I saw several missed calls and texts from Mateo.

Where are you? 911

Alex in danger.

I'm at your house.

"It's Mateo," I said, running toward the door. Confirming it through the peephole, I swung it open. "What's going on?"

"We don't have time," Mateo said. "The Locos are coming for him."

Alex jumped to his feet. "Now? They're coming now?"

Mateo nodded. "We have to go. Get in the car."

Alex didn't argue or even stop to put on his sneakers. He grabbed them and ran out the door.

"Are you sure?" I asked Mateo.

His look answered my question.

RUN

MATEO PUT PEDAL TO METAL. He glanced in the rearview mirror at Alex. "They think you're the snitch."

"*What?* What do you mean?"

"The Locos think one of their own snitched about the shipment."

"And they think it's me?" Alex shrieked.

"Since you left the gang right after, yeah."

"Is it because you helped him that night?" I asked, horrified. "If they think he was hanging with a Destino . . ."

"Nobody saw me help him. It was a total shitstorm. No one could be sure."

"Oh God," Alex said. "I knew Animale was pissed, so I cut

him off. I knew they'd wanna kick my ass but . . . they're gonna kill me."

"No, they won't," Mateo said. "We're not gonna let them near you."

"Where are we going?" Alex asked.

"Atlanta." Mateo checked his mirrors and changed to the fast lane. "To your dad's girlfriend's. You'll have to lay low there until things calm down."

"Okay," Alex said. "Whatever you think."

"You should contact your dad," Mateo said to me. "Let him know we're coming."

"I don't know if he's on the road or at Carol Ann's for the weekend." I called Dad, but his phone was off. I left him a message saying we'd decided to take a spontaneous road trip to Atlanta. We'd tell him the truth later.

"Can you get me her address?" Mateo asked.

"I'll find it," I said, looking for an Atlanta phone book online. I didn't know how Carol Ann would react when we showed up on her doorstep, but it was probably our best option. Dad didn't have much family, just some cousins scattered all over the country. My mom's family, the Hernandezes, were mostly in Jacksonville, but that would be the natural place for the Locos to look for Alex. All they'd need to do was glance at his Facebook page to spot our Jacksonville relatives. I was suddenly glad I'd never added Carol Ann as a friend.

"What if they find me there?" Alex said.

"They won't. Your dad wouldn't be listed at his girlfriend's address. He doesn't have a Facebook page or anything that would connect him to her."

It sounded like Mateo had thought this through. He must've known this could happen.

"None of the Locos know your dad's girlfriend's last name, right?" Mateo asked.

"Right," Alex said. "I don't even know it. I never talked about Dad or Carol Ann to them."

"It's Watkins," I said, looking down at my phone. There were a dozen "C. Watkins" in Atlanta. I knew she lived in the suburb of Brookhaven, so I decided to Google Maps each address to see if one fit.

"The Locos aren't super sly," Mateo said. "They don't have the brains or resources to find you. We just have to get you out of town until the smoke clears."

But would it clear? Would Alex ever be safe in Miami? I wouldn't ask, though. Not now.

"How'd you know they were coming after me?" Alex asked, hugging himself in the backseat. Funny how fear made you cold. The AC wasn't even on, but I was covered in goose bumps.

"Word on the street," Mateo said.

"Bullshit," Alex said. "There *is* a snitch in the Locos, isn't there? That's how you knew they were coming for me. Must be the same person who ratted out the shipment. I guess he told you they were coming after me tonight."

I shot Alex a look. "Let it go."

"Who's the snitch? I really want to know."

"You know I can't tell you." He glared in the rearview mirror. "Don't even think about telling Animale there's a snitch."

Alex looked offended. "I wouldn't rat somebody out to save my own skin."

"Are you sure about that?" Mateo said. "I swear to God, you'd better keep your mouth shut. I'm not helping you just to get my friend killed. If it weren't for him, you could be dead right now. Remember that."

"I'd never give up the snitch," Alex said. "Even if I knew his name. Which I don't."

Mateo gave him a fierce look in the rearview mirror. "And you never will."

At three thirty a.m., we stopped at the Blue Pine Motel off the interstate.

I'd found Carol Ann's address an hour ago—she was the only C. Watkins with a Brookhaven address. If I was wrong, well, we'd wait in Brookhaven until we heard from Dad.

I was glad Mateo was taking a break to sleep. It wasn't

safe for him to drive all night. Besides, it was clear we weren't being followed. The Locos would have no idea where we'd gone.

The door chimed as we walked in. The fat guy at the front desk was watching something intently on his laptop. He slapped it shut.

"A room please," Mateo said.

"Seventy-two eighty."

Mateo paid in cash while I dug into my handbag. "Save it," he said. "We might need it tomorrow."

"Do you have any toiletries?" I asked the guy behind the desk.

He gave me a flat look. "There's shampoo and soap in the room. That's all."

I expected the room to gross me out, but it wasn't bad, despite the dated floral decor. There was a double bed, a TV, and a couch. I threw back the blanket, not spotting any bugs.

"I gotta go." Alex hurried to the bathroom.

"I'll take the couch," Mateo said, smothering a yawn. In the background, we could hear Alex peeing up a storm.

"No way," I said. "You're twice the size of the couch. Plus, you're driving. You're the one who has to be alert, not us. I'll take that couch."

"No, *I* will," Alex said, emerging from the bathroom. He grabbed a blanket from the closet and stretched out on the couch. "I ain't sleeping next to a dude."

"Your loss," Mateo said, a twinkle in his tired eyes.

I took my turn in the bathroom, wishing I at least had a toothbrush. When I came out, the lights were off, and Alex was curled up on the couch.

I didn't see how I was going to fall asleep beside Mateo. He was lying there, shirt off, the covers tucked under his arms. In the predawn gray, his skin looked dark and swarthy against the white sheets. For the first time, I saw the full tattoo on his shoulder, a cursive *R*—the Los Reyes tattoo. After what that gang had done to him, it must be horrible to still be inked with their symbol.

As I slid under the covers, I noticed that he'd kept his jeans on. Probably uncomfortable, but out of respect for me. I peeled off my cardigan and threw it on a chair—I'd sleep in my leggings and T-shirt. I smelled a bit sweaty. Not surprising, since I hadn't had the chance to shower before we fled for our lives.

"I haven't slept in a day and a half," he muttered.

"Why?"

"I don't remember."

My heart sighed. I wanted to touch him, even just to brush a bit of curling dark hair from his eyes. But I wouldn't touch him, of course. I barricaded myself with covers.

I only wished I could barricade my heart. We couldn't ever be together, and his coming to our rescue tonight wouldn't change that. But I still wanted him with a passion that made me ache inside. I didn't know how to stop it.

His eyes were closing, but I wished he would open them and look at me. His face was a bit smooshed against the pillow, scarred side up. I wanted to trace it with my fingers, to love the dark, painful side of him. I wished I could understand why he had to join a gang after he'd lost so much to another one.

"You put yourself on the line for us again," I whispered. "I owe you."

"Don't worry about it," he mumbled.

"I hope you know how much we appreciate—"

He suddenly grabbed me and pulled me against him. I reeled in shock. I thought he was half-asleep, drifting into dreamland. Clearly, I was wrong.

His lips hovered over mine, and my mouth opened in surprise. He took the opportunity to brush his lips against mine. I felt my insides liquefy.

"My brother—"

"Is snoring like a fiend."

It was true. Beyond the sounds of our breaths, I could hear him snoring. Mateo rolled on top of me, his big body covering mine. Heat flooded through me.

"As if I could sleep next to you," he whispered in my ear.

We kissed. Slowly, breathlessly, deeply, only breaking apart to breathe. I told myself this was a bad idea—that we were only torturing ourselves. But I kissed him back with an intensity I couldn't control. An electric current shot through my blood, threatening to cut off power to my brain.

A kiss wouldn't bridge the gulf between us. It wouldn't heal the broken trust or bring us back together. And yet it felt so damned good. Why not enjoy what was probably my last chance to feel his lips on mine?

I'd already lost him, I told myself. So there was nothing to lose.

His kiss was deep, hungry. Our bodies were hot liquid metal ready to fuse. But we didn't do more than kiss. I couldn't, not with my brother a few feet away. But if he hadn't been there? Would I have been able to resist doing more?

The things Mateo was whispering in my ear were killing me. "Do you know how much I want you? How long I've wanted you?"

I said nothing back. He could tell how much I wanted him. I was kissing him so intensely I kept forgetting to breathe. But he didn't need to know that I was still in love with him—that I'd never fallen out of love, as much as I'd tried. I had to keep that part of me safe, secret.

I didn't know how long we kissed in the darkness, straining against each other, breathing each other's breath. Eventually he rolled onto his back. "Cold shower," he said, then went into the bathroom. Seconds later, I heard the shower running.

I huddled under the covers, burying my feelings deep inside me.

When he came back a few minutes later, my back was to him, and I pretended to sleep. I felt him gently stroke my hair, then I heard the slow rhythm of his breathing.

I woke up five minutes later. At least, that's what it felt like. I'd been awake for ages, body burning, before drifting off, long past dawn.

I sat up, rubbing my eyes. Alex was pulling his sweatpants on, yawning.

Mateo came out of the bathroom wearing jeans but no shirt. His hip bones jutted out from his lean, muscular body. God, being so near him was torture. He scrounged around on the bed, finally locating his T-shirt.

"My turn," I said, heading for the shower.

I cringed when I saw my wild hair and scream-queen makeup in the mirror. Turning on the shower, I stripped as I waited for it to warm up. I got in and scrubbed my whole body with soap. But I couldn't wash off the feel of Mateo on my skin—and didn't want to.

Afterward, I rinsed out my mouth and pulled my hair back into a water-slick ponytail. With no makeup or toothbrush, it was the best I could do.

Since we were all famished, we went to the greasy spoon

next door. We each ordered the full breakfast, with coffee for Mateo and me, and OJ for Alex. I checked my phone.

"I got a text from Dad," I said. "'I'm here this weekend. Yes, that's the address. Carol Ann is excited to meet you. See you later. Hope everything is ok.'" I looked at Alex. "We'll have to tell him the truth."

Alex chewed his lower lip. "Not everything, right? We could just say that a gang is after me. We don't need to say that I was hanging out with them. He always said if I joined a gang he'd beat my ass."

"I *wish* he'd been around to beat your ass. He already knows you were hanging out with the Locos. I told him when you got out of the hospital."

Alex glared at me. "You're not serious."

I glared back. "I wasn't going to cover for you. Why should I? Anyway, I told him you were done with the gang."

"Good." He looked at Mateo. "How long do you think I'll have to stay at Carol Ann's?"

"I don't know."

Alex sighed. "I was hoping to pass a few of my classes, at least woodworking and art. Now I'm screwed."

I put a hand over his. "I'll contact the school and see if there's a way to finish some of your courses."

"You will?"

"I'll ask them."

"Nobody can know where he's living, not even his teachers," Mateo said. "Too risky."

Alex looked upset by that, but I said quickly, "Don't worry. Worst comes to worst, you'll redo your courses online like I've been doing. It's not a bad deal. You can work whenever you feel like it and you don't have to go to class."

"All right."

We finished eating, and Mateo paid with cash.

The car needed gas. Mateo insisted on paying for that, too. "I got this," he said, pulling out his wallet again.

"But you got—"

"Don't worry, it's not a problem," he said.

Why was that? I wondered. Was it because he was making money with the Destinos? I knew that he wasn't getting paid as a paramedic yet and that he wasn't making much at the theater. The Destinos had stopped a gun and drug shipment after all—who knew what cut of the profits he got?

But at this point I didn't care where he was getting his money. All I cared about was that he was bringing Alex to safety.

SAFE HAVEN

CAROL ANN WAS A HEAVYSET woman with a brassy poof of blond hair and a cute Georgia twang. She smooshed us into her arms like long-lost friends. I wasn't sure whether to be open to her warmth or wary of it. But I was glad for the friendly welcome, especially for Alex's sake.

She had a big Southern-style house with a wraparound porch and freshly painted white fences. I bet it was Dad who was maintaining it all so nicely. The garden was full of colorful flowers and perfectly trimmed shrubs.

I wondered what they had together, he and Carol Ann. Did he love her?

Dad wore khaki slacks and a button-down shirt. Carol Ann must have laid out the clothes for him. He gave Mateo a *nice to see you* nod, then headed for the trunk. "I'll grab your bags."

"There aren't any," I said. "Let's go in and talk."

The inside of the house didn't disappoint. It was country elegant with lots of charming touches—wicker baskets and picture frames, fresh flowers, monogrammed pillows she'd probably stitched herself. Above the mirror in the foyer was a sign: "Home is where the heart is."

I had a feeling Alex would be comfortable here.

After washing up, we sat down at the dining-room table. It was set with white china, navy cloth napkins, and polished silverware. The centerpiece was a vase of daisies. This Southern hospitality thing wasn't a joke.

Lunch was soup, crusty bread, cold cuts, and sweet tea. Carol Ann went back and forth from the kitchen. When she finally sat down, she asked us to bow our heads for grace.

Dad had told us she was religious. I glanced at him—he bent his head as she said the blessing. I wondered if Carol Ann knew he was an atheist. Anyway, he was smart enough not to bite the hand that feeds him.

The food looked delicious, and my stomach rumbled in response. We passed the dishes around. Dad didn't wait long before asking, "Why no luggage?"

I glanced at Alex.

"Fine," Alex said. "I screwed up big-time. I was hanging

around with a group of assho—bad people, I mean. They're kind of after me right now. Mateo helped get me out of Miami."

Dad's eyes narrowed. "They're *kind of* after you?"

"Alex has to stay out of Miami for a while, so he doesn't get hurt," Mateo said.

Carol Ann pressed a hand to her large chest. "Should we call the police?"

Mateo shook his head. "It won't do any good. It'll only provoke the gang if the cops pay them a visit."

"Gang? These are gang people?" Carol Ann looked horrified.

Religious and *sheltered*, I thought. Great.

"They don't know anything about you or where you live," Mateo assured her. "This is the best place for Alex, if it's okay with you."

"Of course," Carol Ann said without hesitation. "Of course he can stay." She looked at him with compassion, like he was a kid who'd skinned his knee.

Dad was shaking his head. "I can't believe this." He turned to Alex for more explanation, but Alex just hung his head.

"He understands the mistakes he's made," Mateo said, politician smooth. "I'm sure he'll be more careful about who he hangs out with in the future."

"I hope so," Dad said, not taking his eyes off Alex.

A tight silence descended.

"Would anyone like some cobbler?" Carol Ann asked.

"Yes, please," I said.

Carol Ann didn't look ready to kick us out, and for that, I was grateful. I tried to figure out what she saw in my dad. He wasn't a bad-looking man, I supposed. He was a quiet, easygoing sort of person. Dad had no game. He wasn't the charming, cheater type. He could also fix things. He didn't cook but always appreciated it when somebody cooked for him.

Actually it sounded like Dad wasn't a bad match for Carol Ann. I suspected she doted on him, cooked great meals, and did his laundry. Bet she didn't nag him too much.

A sweet deal for both of them.

It was strange, seeing him with a woman other than my mom. But it wasn't as weird as I'd imagined. I used to worry that he'd be alone for the rest of his life. I'd never wanted that for him. Besides, something about Carol Ann was . . . soothing.

Once we'd finished our cobbler, Carol Ann took us on a minitour of the house. She'd inherited it from her mother's family, she said—which explained why she owned such a nice place on a teacher's pay. She showed us upstairs to the bedrooms. There were three guest rooms, one for each of us. The rooms looked freshly cleaned, the beds made up with masses of lace-edged pillows.

"Thanks for the hospitality, Ms. Watkins," Mateo said. "It's nice of you to take us in on short notice. I'll be leaving early in the morning."

"Me too," I said.

Mateo looked at me sharply but didn't say anything.

Afterward, Mateo and Alex went to watch TV in the basement. I could picture my dad putting up his feet on the coffee table and lounging on the comfy couch, watching a game on the big screen. I went out to the porch with him and Carol Ann. She served up a sparkling peach drink.

"Do you really have to leave tomorrow?" Carol Ann said, sitting down on a wicker chair. "I hope not. Y'all just got here."

"I wish I could stay, but I have to work. I took time off after Alex was hurt."

"But are *you* safe from those gang people?"

I hadn't even thought of that. I'd been too busy worrying about Alex. "I think so. Alex is the one they're after. We don't know how long he'll need to stay away. It could be a while. I hope it's not too much trouble for him to stay here, especially since my dad's away so much." I bit my lip. Visiting Dad's girlfriend was one thing—moving Alex into her house was another.

"It's no trouble at all." Carol Ann looked like she wanted to say more, but then turned to my dad. "Marc."

There was a long pause. Dad cleared his throat, squirming a bit. "We're getting married."

"Wow." I blinked, forcing a smile. I wasn't sure how to react to the news, but it felt important not to hurt Carol Ann's feelings. "That's great! When'd this happen?"

"Last month," Carol Ann said apologetically. "I'm sorry if this is a shock. I've been wanting to meet you and your brother for months, but I guess the stars haven't lined up."

The stars haven't lined up was just another way of saying that my dad hadn't made it happen. It was nice of her not to throw him under the bus, but I wouldn't blame her if she had. Dad obviously felt uncomfortable introducing a new woman to us, so he'd done what he does best—simply avoided it. The man had avoidance down to a science.

Dad couldn't even look at me now, didn't dare smile at his own announcement.

I took a sip of my drink, feeling the sweetness burst in my mouth. "I'm so happy for you guys. This is exciting."

Carol Ann smiled. "Thanks, Grace. That means the world."

"Have you set a date yet?"

"We were thinking of Thanksgiving weekend. It's only four months away, but I think that's enough time to work out the details. I'd love for you to be involved in planning the wedding, if you'd like."

"I'd be happy to."

* * *

Mateo and I set out early the next morning. Putting in earbuds, I listened to my favorite playlist, trying to zone out. But it didn't work. Memories of Saturday night in the motel room flashed through my brain. An infrared light would probably pick up the sparks of heat between us, along with the ice-cold patches of distance.

Halfway through the trip, we stopped at Subway.

He took a few bites of his footlong, then set it down, eyeing me. "You okay?"

"Okay about what? The fact that my dad's marrying someone I just met or that Alex's life is in danger?"

"Both."

I shrugged. "I like her. Hell, I might like her more than I like my own dad. So I'm okay with it. I just hope Alex is." They'd announced the news at dinner last night. Alex had looked shocked, but not upset, exactly. We hadn't had the chance to debrief about it afterward—not that he'd share his feelings with me anyway.

"It could be a good thing," Mateo said. "Alex will be more comfortable there knowing it's a done deal between them."

I nodded, eating some baked chips.

"As for the other thing." His eyes met mine. "The Locos aren't coming after you, in case you're worried."

"Who said I was worried?"

"No one. I just want you to know that if anyone talks about coming after you, I'll hear about it."

I broke a large chip in half. "Because of the snitch. He keeps you informed."

"Yeah. He's high up in the gang."

"Comforting." I ate some of my sub, then wiped my mouth with a napkin. "If you ever get the chance, thank him for me. He took a risk warning us."

He nodded grimly. "If somebody had figured it out, he'd be dead already. But nobody did."

"Good. I don't want him to get hurt, whoever he is."

"Me neither. I tried to talk him out of infiltrating the Locos in the first place. Even our leader thought it was a crazy plan. But he insisted."

"I wonder why."

Mateo sighed. "He's got a death wish. Has to do with things he did in the past, or didn't do. Guess he thinks if he can save other people, he can make it right. I don't know. Anyway, you don't need to be scared. He'll keep us informed."

"That's good." I sipped my soda. "I'm not scared for myself, just for Alex."

"They won't go crazy looking for him. He's not worth it."

"I hope you're right."

"I'm right, trust me."

I must've made a doubtful sound, because he said, "What?"

"I do trust you." I splayed my hands. "But I have no idea why, considering I don't even understand you. I thought I did for a while there, but I was fooling myself."

"I know." He held my gaze, and a ripple of connection passed between us. "I don't expect you to understand why I'm a Destino. You probably think I'm a hypocrite after what I said about the Reyes."

I didn't respond. He knew what my answer would be.

He fisted his napkin. "It's been hard enough losing you, Grace. But losing your respect is worse. Maybe I can make you understand."

"You can try."

"I met a few of the Destinos in juvie. They weren't Destinos then, just a group of guys who got together for protection. Those first few weeks, I was afraid for my life. It was like a microcosm of the street, everybody shoved in together like rats. Fights every day. Being a Reyes helped at times, but it also made some people hate me on sight. Anyway, there was this guy named X. Nobody knew his real name or his story. He invited me to join up with his guys. Normally he said he wouldn't bring in a gang member, but he could tell I was cool."

"I see."

"I was in juvie for six months, and it took a while before I got out of the Reyes . . . and then, the hospital. But eventually I met up with X and the guys again. They'd formed a group that helped girls who'd been forced into the sex trade. They were righting wrongs. Helping people. They knew how I'd stood up to Toro, knew the Reyes had called me 'Matador.' The name stuck." He looked up, trying to gauge my thoughts. "The Destinos needed me."

"So you wanted to help them, since they'd helped you."

"Yeah, but nobody pressured me. With the risks involved, they only wanted people who were sure about joining."

"And you were sure."

A bleak look came into his eyes. "I had nothing else to live for."

My heart hurt for him. It was hard to imagine how low he must've been back then. He'd lost everything. "What about now?"

"It's different now. I've got a future. A career. My own place and my own car. But I couldn't have gotten back on track without them."

"I get it." His choices, at least, made sense now. "Thanks for telling me."

He was studying me. "I guess it doesn't change anything for us."

My heart thumped against my rib cage. It *had* changed something. His choice to join the Destinos didn't seem so crazy anymore. It seemed rational. I took a breath. "You mentioned the risks involved. Are those risks you think I'd be okay with?"

His gaze darted away from mine. I could tell he didn't like my question. "No, I guess not."

"Then it doesn't change anything," I said. Could it never get easier between us?

The flicker of hope in his eyes died out. "Guess we'd better hit the road."

THE GIFT

THE NEXT MORNING I DRAGGED myself out of bed, downed two cups of coffee, applied makeup to try to look human, and took a bus to Compass.

It was a rare overcast day. The sun had stayed in bed, and I wished I had too. I felt totally drained. As much as I wanted to see the kids, not to mention Kylie and Yolanda, I didn't want to bring everyone down.

But the strangest thing happened when I walked in the doors.

Somebody yelled, "Gwaaaace!"

A group of kids rushed at me, arms wide.

I bent down to receive their hugs, and I remembered

what I'd learned on many dreary days: the kids could always lift me up.

After several hugs and kisses and *I missed you*s, Yolanda approached me. "How's your brother?"

"He's doing better." I gave her a look that said, *It's complicated. It's ongoing.* Yolanda nodded sympathetically and didn't ask for more details.

"Where's Sofia?" I asked, looking around.

"Safe space." Yolanda gestured toward the toy cottage in the corner of the room, full of stuffed animals. Kids could go there if they ever needed some time alone—or if they felt sad or scared. While some kids were lap kids, crawling onto one of us for comfort, others preferred have their own space.

"Has she been spending a lot of time in there?" I asked, frowning.

"More than usual since you've been away, but she's all right," Yolanda said.

I went up to Sofia, knocking on the small red door of the cottage. "Look who's back."

She didn't say anything. I couldn't tell if she was happy to see me.

Damn it. All that progress.

"Did Yolanda tell you how much I missed you last week?" I whispered.

She nodded, holding on to her favorite stuffed animal, a purple teddy bear with big ears that she liked to whisper into.

"Did anybody tell you why I wasn't here last week?"

She shook her head.

"My brother got hurt. He had a big boo-boo right here." I touched my head. "I had to take care of him so he would get better. Do you understand?"

She nodded.

"Would you like to come to circle time now? Kylie's about to start a story. I think it's the one about the bear who lost his underwear."

Was that a glimmer of curiosity? A spark of something?

I reached out. "Will you hold my hand?"

She looked at my hand, then at me. Her tiny fingers slipped into mine, and I breathed a sigh of relief.

Instead of having Alex at home all the time, I was alone now. But there was peace in being alone. There was no one to cook for or clean up after. I didn't have to worry about him going to school. Most of all, I didn't have to worry about him doing God-knows-what with the Locos. He was safe in Atlanta with Carol Ann and Dad.

I studied, uninterrupted, for my sociology exam and ended up with an A in the course. With that final mark submitted, I just had to wait to find out whether I'd be accepted into the ECE program next year.

I called Alex every other night, and he seemed happy to chat. He liked Carol Ann's cooking and was amazed at the overstuffed fridge. The neighborhood was nice and safe, and she'd even got him a membership at a kickboxing gym. True, he found Carol Ann nosy, and he didn't like being asked to clean up after himself. But all in all, it sounded like he was enjoying Atlanta. He had more life in his voice than he'd had in a while.

Although he'd never admit it, I suspected he missed me.

I missed him, too.

Two weeks after Alex's escape from Miami, Animale posted on Alex's Facebook page: *Fuck da snitch, karma's a bitch.*

I'd been sitting watching TV when I saw it pop up on his page. I called him right away.

"You've got to freeze your pages. All of them. Now."

He was silent for a while. "There's no point in freezing them. I'll delete them."

"I think that's a good idea."

We both knew what that meant. It meant letting go of his past. He'd been crafting his identity on those pages for years. In one click, they'd be gone.

"I need to disappear," he said. "*Santo* needs to disappear." There was a quiet certainty in his voice. "It's the only way."

"I'm really proud of you."

"Thanks. Hang on a sec. I'm deleting the pages right now."

I stayed on the phone with him as he did it.

Afterward, he let out a breath. "Done. And, Grace?"

"Yeah?"

"How'd you see what Animale put on my Facebook page? I blocked you."

"I have my ways."

"Seriously. How'd you see it?"

"Will you be mad if I tell you?"

"No."

"You know that gorgeous girl who friended you a few months ago, Alexandra Chen? It's a picture of my friend Kylie from Compass. I created the profile and sent you a friend request. Sorry, but your weakness for smokin' hot girls was your downfall."

He laughed. "You catfished me!"

"I did what I had to do."

"You owe it to me to introduce us one day."

"Sure. But she's too old for you."

That night, I decided to write a poem about evil, about the many faces it wears. While I was writing, I had Animale in mind. The first time I met him, I caught the scent of a predator. It was too bad Alex had mistaken him for a friend.

Seconds after I finished the poem, a text came up from Mateo: Smart to take down the pages.

So he'd been monitoring Alex's social media too. I shouldn't be surprised. Mateo was always looking out for us.

My heart ached. Since our talk on the way back from Atlanta, part of me wondered if I should try to accept that he was in the gang. But whenever I thought about it, a wave of anxiety came over me. Could I spend my days and nights worrying about him? Is that what I wanted for myself?

No matter how many times I asked myself those questions, the answer was always no.

I'd spent the last year desperate to regain control over my own life. And now, with Alex safe in Atlanta, it was finally happening. Independence was within my grasp. If all went well, I'd be going to college in September. I couldn't put my future at risk to be with a gang member, no matter how much I loved him.

And I couldn't help but think that if he loved me enough, he wouldn't ask it of me.

"You haven't forgotten what Monday night is, have you?" Feenix asked me the following Thursday at work.

I thought about it. "It's not your birthday, is it?"

She rolled her eyes.

"Enlighten me."

"It's the last poetry slam of the year! Our top three finalists are going to the city finals."

"Oh." I swallowed nervously. I hadn't presented a poem last Monday and I'd missed the adrenaline rush. Although my poem was ready for next week, I wasn't sure I wanted to be part of a competition.

"I was going to do a poem about evil," I said.

"I know you like dark poetry, but evil?" She gave me a scrutinizing look. "You doing okay, sweetie?"

I waved away her concern. "I'm fine." She knew I was grieving Mateo. We'd talked about it a lot over the last couple of weeks. Nothing new there.

"Well, evil can be awesome. I mean, in poetry. Not in real life. I can't wait to hear your poem."

"I'm not sure if it's good enough for a competition. Want to hear a couple of lines?" I took out my phone.

"Hell, no." She put up her hands. "Don't spoil it for me. You know it's good enough. Don't you dare doubt yourself."

"All right." I put my phone away. "Do you have a poem ready?"

"Not yet. The Muse will speak to me when she's ready."

"The Muse, huh? Sounds spiritual."

"Poetry *is* spiritual. It should be a registered freaking religion—the only religion I'd ever sign up for. Haven't you figured that out by now?"

"I hadn't thought of it that way."

"We don't write poems, Grace. We intercept them. We pluck them from the universe." She reached into the air, as if picking an apple off a tree.

I raised my eyebrows, not sure if she was messing with me.

"Call it what you want. Hokey. New Agey. Quackers. Poetry's not about stringing one word with another so it sounds pretty. It's about channeling the truth. It might be *my* truth or a truth that doesn't make sense to anybody but the guy with purple hair in the back row. But poetry rings true for someone. We're just the messengers."

"I think you're right."

"You *know* I'm right."

"Have you thought about writing a poem about writing poems?"

She shrugged. "Maybe I will. Let's see what the Muse sends me."

I smiled. Reason number 562 why Feenix was awesome.

Later that night, Luke called me into his office. He sat behind his desk, looking damned proud of himself.

"What's got you grinning?" I asked.

"Nothing much . . . except *this*." He handed me a small envelope. I slipped what looked like tickets out of it. My jaw dropped.

Two Pitbull tickets. Box seats.

"Holy, you're so lucky! How'd you score these?"

He shook his head. "No, *you're* so lucky. They're for you. You haven't exactly made your love of Pitbull a secret around here."

"But these must've cost—"

He put up a hand. "They didn't cost me a thing. A friend of mine owns a security company. When he told me he was doing the Pitbull concert, I asked if he could hook me up."

I paused for a second. This gift was awesome—*too* awesome. Should I refuse to accept it? He wasn't trying to reel me in, was he?

He must've sensed my confusion. "There are no strings. Take a friend. Have fun. I know it's been a tough time for you. And, Grace, I want you to know that I'm sorry for . . . *you know*. I really am. I hope we'll always be friends."

"Me too." I got a bit teary-eyed. "Thanks, Luke. This is so nice of you."

His eyes lit up. "It's worth it for your smile. There's one catch, though." He took something from his drawer, and put two gold badges on his desk.

"Backstage passes?"

"Yes. The catch is that I want a picture of you with Pitbull to put on the wall. Don't be shy. I hear he's a really chill guy."

"I'll do my best."

* * *

"Make it count," Feenix coached me before the show. "Don't forget, only three people make the city finals."

"Two," I said. "You're a shoo-in."

Her mouth kicked up at one side. I envied her confidence.

She'd better make the finals. If she didn't, there would probably be a riot.

I stood at the back of Oz Kafé, scanning the room. There was a bigger than usual crowd tonight. Until that moment, I'd told myself I didn't care about making the city finals. But suddenly I did.

When my turn came, I walked to the front and felt something I hadn't felt in a long time: optimism. Maybe I could do this.

I could at least try.

"A little something I'm working on," I said, testing my voice in the microphone. I didn't look directly at the judges, but Feenix had pointed them out to me—three hipsters at the back, two girls and a guy. I felt them look up.

They say you can tell
Evil
By its smell
The hideous funk

Of sweet cologne.
They say you can tell
Deceit
By the twinkle of green eyes
The curl of its lips
The flash of brilliant teeth.

They say you can spot the lie
By its vague explanation
Its clever redirection
The twist of your gut.

And you
You are a master of those ways
You wear the guise of a friend
Kindly
Gladly
Plotting my damnation.

Pause, breathe, smile. The applause started.

I didn't look at the judges. I didn't need their approval. I'd delivered my poem the best I knew how.

Which meant I'd already won.

I went over to sit with Feenix and Kenny. She gave me a *you killed it* fist pump.

An hour later, Feenix did too. She killed it.

It was after eleven by the time the last poet performed. I was nearly sprawled across the table with tiredness. There were too many poets tonight. Even the half-assed ones, the ones who rarely showed up, came tonight hoping to make the finals.

As the judges deliberated, Feenix shifted in her seat. She wanted this badly.

The judge with frizzy red hair and glasses stepped up behind the mike. "Shhh, everyone. Thanks for your patience. There is an incredible amount of talent in this room and this has been a very tough decision for us. But only three can make the finals. So here is the first one: Grace Dillane."

The crowd whooped, many of them turning my way and clapping. Feenix squeezed my shoulder. I couldn't believe it. Me? Had I seriously just made the finals?

"The next finalist is Colton Thomas."

I felt Feenix tense beside me, and my heart pounded in my ears. She *had* to make the finals. If she didn't, we'd all freak. She deserved it more than anyone.

Dear God, if I made it and she didn't, I wouldn't be able to live with myself. I wouldn't even be here without her. She was ten times the poet I was. She was—

The red-haired judge was speaking, ". . . but certainly not least, Feenix Menzies."

The crowd hoorayed.

"Hells yeah!" I said, and hugged her. We'd both made it, thank God!

We didn't stick around to celebrate. As we headed out to Kenny's car, a black Mazda pulled up, the windows rolled down.

The sight of Mateo made my heart leap. But the grim look on his face made my stomach drop. Something was wrong.

"I'll drive you home."

"Sure, thanks. Talk to you guys later," I said, slipping into the passenger seat before Feenix could question me.

As soon as he started to drive, I turned to him. "Is this about Alex? Do they know where he is?"

"No, don't worry. I just wanted to talk to you."

About us? I wondered. I allowed myself a moment of hope. Had he decided to leave the gang?

"I liked your poem," he said. "I'm not surprised you made the finals."

"You were there? I didn't see you."

"I didn't want to distract you."

"What makes you think you'd distract me?"

We exchanged a look, and my mouth went dry. "I'm glad you liked it. I was thinking about Alex's situation when I wrote it. About enemies who masquerade as friends, like Animale." I shuddered. "But I have the feeling you didn't show up tonight to watch my poetry. What did you want to talk about?"

He sobered. "I think we should wait until I get you home."

I knew then that he hadn't come to me tonight with a change of heart. I should've sensed it already—his body language was closed off, his vibe tense. I felt a rush of disappointment.

When we got to my place, Mateo came in and sat on the couch across from me. I took in his lean, strong physique, every detail of muscle and bone and weary brown eyes. I wondered if there would ever be a time when he wouldn't affect me this way—when I wouldn't resent the space between us.

He raked a hand through his hair. "I heard about Luke's gift."

I blinked. Was *that* what this was about? Another warning about Luke the player?

"He knows I love Pitbull, and one of his friends is working security." I put my hands up before he could speak. "But I can't be bought, and he's not stupid enough to think I can."

"I know. But it's not good enough. I've decided I can't risk it."

"Risk what?"

His eyes met mine. "You getting involved with Luke."

"I'm not," I said, exasperated. "But even if I wanted to, it's none of your business."

A muscle in his jaw twitched. "I wish it were my business, but you're right. It isn't. Still, I should tell you what I know about him."

"What you know?" I frowned. "Everybody knows he's an ex-con. His past isn't a secret."

"I'm talking about his present."

"Excuse me?"

"Luke is crooked. At least, we think he is."

"What are you talking about?"

His gaze didn't stray from mine. "That's why I started working at the theater. The Destinos are investigating him."

The world shifted around me. Mateo was investigating Luke? It didn't make any sense.

"Luke's old gang, the Brothers-in-Arms, have a smuggling ring," Mateo said. "We think he's laundering money for them."

"What?"

Something clicked in my mind. Mateo hadn't been in Luke's office that night looking for cash, after all. He'd been trying to find dirt on our boss.

"Luke would never launder money for them or for anyone," I said. "He's worked too hard to get where he is to risk going back to jail."

"You don't know that. The Brothers-in-Arms are a sick, twisted group. Remember the massacre last year in Jacksonville where five guys got hacked up in a roadside diner?"

I nodded, my arms circling my queasy stomach. It had been all over the news.

"That was the Brothers-in-Arms teaching a rival biker gang a lesson. We're trying to shut them down. But we need to figure out where they're laundering their money."

"It's not your job to shut them down," I said. "Leave it to the police. The FBI. Whoever."

"We're not totally on our own."

"Are you working with the cops?"

He said nothing, but that was as good as confirming it.

"You're insane, Mateo. Whether Luke's involved or not— and I'm sure he isn't—the Destinos can't possibly take on a biker gang. Going after the Locos is bad enough." I flashed back to news clips of the aftermath of the massacre, and shuddered. The Brothers-in-Arms were monsters.

"We can take them on," he said with quiet confidence. "All the evidence points to Luke doing the laundering through the theater. Where does an ex-con find the money to buy a movie theater in the first place?"

"Maybe he got a loan like regular people do. I don't know."

He gave me a *come on* look.

"I know Luke," I said. "He's not a saint, but he's a decent person. A *kind* person. He's learned from his mistakes. He wouldn't have anything to do with the Brothers-in-Arms."

Mateo looked mystified. "Why are you taking this so personally?"

"I—I just told you why."

His gaze flickered. "Did something happen between you two?"

I didn't answer. My face flushed.

"When?"

"The night Alex got hurt," I said, feeling ashamed.

Pain burned across his face, but he masked it quickly. "I told you he was dangerous. Why didn't you listen to me?"

"I thought you meant because he was a player! And it's not up to you what I do." *I didn't think you wanted me.*

If only I could do it—reach across, grab his hand. Find a way.

"So you and Luke." He shook his head in disbelief. "Wow."

"It's not what you're thinking. We just kissed. That's it."

"I'm glad to hear that." His eyes were shuttered now, his emotions closed off. "I hope I've convinced you to stay away from him from now on."

"You don't have to convince me of anything. I wasn't going to let it happen again. We agreed it was a total mistake."

He got up. "Make sure you don't let on to Luke that you know anything. I've still got some investigating to do."

I grabbed his arm as he stood up. "Mateo, please. I'm not the one you should be concerned about. What do you think the Brothers-in-Arms would do if they knew you were investigating them? Even if you think it's a good cause, you can't be doing your gang's dirty work."

His expression hardened. "I'm not doing anybody's dirty work. Besides, I volunteered for the job."

I stared at him. "Why would you do that?"

"Because I found out you were working at the theater."

Before I could say anything, he walked out.

MINE

AT THREE A.M., I STILL couldn't sleep. I was furious. I sat up in bed and texted Mateo:

> I can't sleep thanks to you. If you cared about me at all you'd give up your little investigation.

He got back to me within seconds:

> Don't text about it.

I turned off my phone, tempted to throw it across the room. There was no talking him out of this. His loyalty was to the Destinos. He'd do whatever it took to finish the job and nothing I could say would make any difference.

My alarm woke me a few hours later. I hit the snooze button twice, then forced myself to sit up, light-headed from lack of sleep. After a quick shower, I found a couple of granola bars to eat on the bus. I grabbed yesterday's mail on the way out and shoved it into my purse, hoping there weren't any overdue bills.

When I got to Compass, we swim-suited and sun-screened the kids for water play in the backyard. Normally we would've gone to the neighborhood splash pad, but Yolanda was nervous about taking them off-site with the recent shooting. She'd brought in an old Slip'N Slide and two sprinklers. We'd make it work.

On my lunch break, I opened my mail in the staff room. With all the late bills we'd received in the past, I now had mail-opening PTSD. It turned out to be mostly junk mail and a letter from the Miami-Dade Admissions Department.

My stomach tightened. This must be it—my acceptance or rejection letter to the Early Childhood Education program. I took a breath, feeling my nerves tremble. *Whatever the letter says, I'll be okay*, I told myself. I'd deal. *What's meant to be will be.*

I stared at the letter, almost afraid to open it. I'd been working up to this for almost a year. I only hoped all my efforts to get in had been enough.

Tearing open the letter, I scanned it.

I got in!

My head sank to my chest in pure relief. *Thank God.*

I raised my head to continue reading the letter, and my eyes almost popped out of my head. I got a scholarship too! *What?*

Telling myself to calm down, I read the entire letter again to make sure it was real. It was.

My tuition next year would be paid. My grades—and all my volunteer experience—had done it.

My future was finally falling into place.

I thought of Mom. She'd be so proud. She'd always told me to make my life count, and working with children was my way of doing that. Sure, the kids might grow up and forget all the times I'd encouraged and comforted them. But I believed that, on some level, it still made a difference. As Mom said, *Love's never wasted.*

I texted Alex, Dad, and Carol Ann with my big news. I wanted to text Mateo, but there was no point. He was a drug I was going to have to wean off sooner or later.

Carol Ann replied right away: Fabulous news! You'll have to come up soon to celebrate!

Yolanda came into the staff room to grab the veggies from the fridge. I held up the letter. "I got accepted into ECE—and I got a scholarship too!"

Her eyes lit up. "That's wonderful!" She gave me a hug.

"I'm sure it was your recommendation that got me the scholarship."

She waved a hand. "It's *you* that did it. Do you think the other applicants had hundreds of volunteer hours? I don't think so. You're an asset to our program, Grace. I hope you can do at least two of your three placements with us. Now, make sure to put the letter on my desk before you leave today so we can get you started with payroll."

"What? Payroll?"

"Yes." She smiled. "Didn't you know? We can pay our employees who are enrolled in an ECE program. A letter of admission is good enough for payroll. It'll take a couple of weeks to process, but hopefully we can pay you retroactive to the letter's date."

I couldn't believe it. "Wow."

"You work so hard. Sometimes I think you work *too* hard with both your jobs. You deserve to be paid." She lifted the tray of veggies and left the kitchen.

The implications spun in my head. My volunteer work at Compass was turning into a paid job. *And* I'd gotten a scholarship. I felt like I'd won the lottery.

Or something better: independence.

I closed my eyes and let it wash over me. My future was, suddenly, my own.

When my break was over, I found the kids wearing party

hats. For a second I thought it was somebody's birthday. Yolanda and Kylie counted, "One, two, three!" The kids yelled, "Hooway for Gwace!" and started clapping and cheering.

I laughed. Some kids came up for hugs. Sofia was last in line.

"Congwatuwations," she whispered in my ear.

"Thank you." I squeezed her tight.

"It's about freaking time you're getting paid," Kylie said, hugging me. "You're gonna run this place one day, no doubt about it. All I ask is that when you do, I get Fridays off in the summer."

I grinned. "Done."

"You're definitely going to Luke's tonight," Feenix said Saturday at work. "We have to celebrate!"

"I'm in." I hadn't gone to one of his parties in a month, but tonight I felt like celebrating.

I'd posted a selfie holding the acceptance letter, and people had been congratulating me all week. I had to admit, it felt really good.

"You're not going to quit this job once you start school, right?" Feenix asked. "I couldn't rock this pretzel stand with anybody else."

"I'm not going anywhere." In the fall, I'd be juggling

college, teaching placements, and the theater. I'd probably take fewer shifts, but I wouldn't quit. "I like it here. Let's face it, we're being paid to hang out together and we get free pretzels. Not a bad deal."

"Don't you forget that, sweets," she said, giving me a one-armed squeeze.

Customers kept us busy for the next hour. I took my break with a pretzel and a soda. I saw a quick movement, and then Mateo was sitting in front of me.

I felt it—the familiar electric charge of his presence. My hands tingled, and I curled them tightly around my drink. I still couldn't believe he'd been spying on Luke this whole time. Did he have more secrets to lay on me?

Before I could open my mouth to ask, he said quietly, "We're not talking about that here."

I sipped my drink, feeling the iciness flow down my throat. "There's nothing to talk about anyway. You know how I feel."

"And you know how I feel."

I saw the look on his face and realized that we were talking about two different things. I squelched the wave of longing inside me.

"I just wanted to congratulate you," he said.

"You already did. You liked my post on Facebook."

"Right, well, I wanted to do it in person. I'm really glad you got in and got that scholarship. You deserve every good thing that comes your way." His eyes were warm. "I'll always be cheering you on from the sidelines, even if you don't know I'm there."

His words touched me, and I could hardly form a reply. "Thanks."

He managed a half smile, then got up and left me alone.

After Mateo's little speech, there was a lump in my throat that wouldn't go away. Although my need to party had faded, I'd promised Feenix we'd celebrate. Besides, I didn't want to face the emptiness of my house.

I walked over to Luke's with Feenix and Kenny. Eddie, Jamar, Nina, and Nyla were already there. Two trays of hot, gooey nachos were spread out on the breakfast bar. Judging by his bloodshot eyes, Eddie had already started drinking. He offered to pour me one, but I shook my head and grabbed a can of Coke Zero.

"So you got yourself a sweet scholarship, I hear," Eddie said, pulling a few nachos out, cheese stringing in a big line. "Congratulations are in order."

"Thanks."

"I hate to break it to you, but formal education is worthless. Obviously you're good at working with kids. You don't need a paper to confirm it."

"No, but you need the qualification to get paid at Compass."

"That's exactly my point," he said, nachos garbling his speech. "You need to get the diploma just to work where you're *already* working. That's fucked-up." He sipped some beer. "I went to college. Did I ever tell you that?"

"Yes."

"I stopped two credits before finishing. My parents think I did it just to piss them off, but it's not true. It's because I can't stand credentialism and won't play along."

Of course, he expected me to ask what *credentialism* was. There was no need, though. I could figure it out.

He told me anyway. "It's the attitude that if you have a degree, you're better than everybody else. What college you went to is a factor too. My sister went to Vassar and my parents brag about it nonstop. It's just a way for The Man to decide who gets privilege and who gets dick all."

"That's terrible."

Luke and Mateo came in then, laughing about something. There were three hot girls with them.

"Luke's posse," Eddie grumbled.

Mateo saw me right away. He looked almost apologetic, and I could see why. One of the girls was glued to his side. She had beach babe written all over her—skinny like she'd never eaten a burger, with a golden tan, unnaturally black hair and sky-blue eyes.

I looked away, my gut wrenching.

Eddie was still talking to me, and I nodded at the appropriate times. Eventually I told him I had to go to the bathroom, and slipped away.

Over the next half hour, another dozen people arrived and a dance floor started in the living room. Kenny had taken charge of the music, putting on some quality hip-hop and electro soul. Feenix was dancing for him in that cool, sensual way she had, and he was loving every minute. They were happy.

So was the girl currently dancing with Mateo. She had one arm around his neck and was winding it up in front of him. He was looking down, focusing on the gymnastic swirl of her hips. She moved well, I had to admit. Maybe she had some Latina in her.

Mateo's little speech stuck in my mind. If he cared about me so much, did he have to rebound right in front of me?

I wasn't going to join the dancers, not with Mateo among them. So I went back into the kitchen where Luke sat with two hot girls. I pulled up a stool. One of the girls gave me a quick once-over, then lifted her chin, as if deciding that I was no competition.

Luke was telling a story about a childhood encounter with a ghost. He caught me up on the basics before diving in again. "I went to the bathroom in the middle of the night. It was pitch-dark, but my eyes adjusted. I made the mistake of looking in the mirror."

One of the girls clutched his arm. "The old man in the fedora?"

"Yeah. I saw the outline of him behind me, hat and all. But the weird thing was, even though it was dark, I remember seeing the expression in his eyes."

The girl gave a little shriek. "Was he angry at you for disrupting his home?"

"No, nothing like that. His eyes were crinkled like he was worried about me. I think he felt sympathy for me."

"Why?" the girl asked.

His face darkened. "Those were shitty times. My mom had just lost her job and shacked up with a loser. But the worst was to come. Maybe the man in the mirror . . . he knew."

"I think my mom came back once," I said, surprising myself for saying it in front of these people. But Luke's honesty inspired me. "We were packing up her things and I found an old flashlight with no batteries in it. It looked pretty crappy so I threw it in a garbage bag. But when I looked back, it was on, shining through the bag."

"Sounds like she paid you a visit," Luke said.

"I'd like to think so."

I saw Luke glancing down the hallway. Following his gaze, I watched Mateo and that girl slip into the bedroom.

Luke smirked. I gave a shrug, trying to mask my feelings.

Was Mateo really hooking up with her? What the hell?

The girl beside me launched into a ghost story of her own. I spent the next few minutes pretending to listen, but all I wanted to do was cry. I went back to the living room and hung out until Feenix and Kenny decided to leave.

"You okay?" Feenix asked me in the car.

"Not really."

"I guess you saw . . ."

"Everybody saw. It's fine. It's over."

"I didn't think it was classy of him to hook up with a girl with you there. It hasn't been that long since you broke up."

To get technical about it, we hadn't actually been together in four years. But I still wasn't ready for him to rebound.

When we arrived at my house, Feenix got out of the car and gave me a hug. Freaking supportive friend. Tears stung my eyes.

I hurried inside, flicked on the lights, and locked the door.

I didn't think I could stand the emptiness of this house one moment longer.

Heading upstairs, I took a long, hot shower. Tears and water ran down my body. I wanted to be free of Mateo. He was nothing but an anchor on my heart. I wanted to be free of this house. Of the past. Of missing my mom.

I cried harder, until I was all cried out.

After drying off, I put on a long T-shirt and went to bed. It was a hot, sweaty night, and I couldn't sleep with the constant clicking of the ceiling fan. I left the window open, hoping for a breeze that never came.

I jolted awake some time later. My phone was buzzing.

The screen lit up: Mateo.

I picked up. "What?"

"I'm downstairs. Let me in."

"Are you kidding? It's two thirty-seven."

"Let me in, Grace."

"Fine."

I scrubbed a hand over my face and went downstairs. For once, I didn't care if he saw me sleep rumpled and makeup free.

I swung open the door. "Hoping for a second booty call? Didn't know you had it in you."

His dark eyes burned into me. "I guess you didn't figure out why I went to Luke's tonight?"

"I don't know. Maybe you wanted to search his apartment for evidence of his money laundering? Guess you got a little sidetracked."

"I didn't get sidetracked."

"Sure."

He shouldered his way in the door, closing and locking it. "I didn't hook up with that girl. I had to search Luke's bedroom. She was my excuse."

"Poor you." I splayed my hands on his chest. I was furious, but couldn't stop myself from touching him. "Did you have to give your body to the cause? Let her put her hands all over you?"

He sucked in a breath, as if my hands burned him.

"Did she just lie there patiently while you searched his bedroom?"

"She helped me. That's why I brought her."

I closed my eyes, feeling dumb. "Oh. Are you saying she's . . . one of you?"

"Yes."

"Well, kudos to her. She put on quite a show." I drew my hands away. "Did you find anything on Luke?"

"Tonight, no. But I've looked at his books, and I know for sure that the books don't match the bank deposits. That's all I can tell you." He grasped one of my hands, pressing it to his chest again. "Don't stop touching me. It feels good."

"I told you I can't be with you. Didn't you say I deserve better?"

"You do. But it doesn't change how I feel."

The heat of his gaze melted me. Damn him. It wasn't fair to stand here and say that to me. It was torture.

"I always thought you'd be my first, you know," I said. "It didn't work out that way."

I wasn't sure why I said it—maybe to get it off my chest. Maybe to hurt him.

Mateo didn't look surprised. He simply tipped up my

chin. "Maybe I couldn't be your first, but you could be mine."

I blinked. "You're not serious."

"I don't publicize it, but yeah." He blushed. "It's not that bad, is it?"

"No, no. I'm just shocked."

"It might surprise you, but girls haven't been knocking down my door. This is a face only a mother could—"

"Shhh." I put a finger over his lips. "I love your face."

He cleared his throat. "When I had the chance to, you know, I always felt like I'd be betraying you. Any other girl would be a shitty substitute for you. So, no, I didn't do it."

I pressed my head into his chest. My tears were getting his shirt wet, and I didn't care. "I can't believe you're saying . . . you waited for me. I wish you hadn't."

"Don't regret your past. I don't regret mine. I always planned to come back to you, Grace. You might think I should have when I got out of the Reyes, but I couldn't. I promised myself I wasn't gonna come back to you broken. You needed me whole or not at all."

He was right about that. I needed him whole.

"Last year, once I'd started college, I felt like I was ready," he said. "I finally had my shit together. But I did my research and found out you had a boyfriend. Some jock named Ben. I heard you were happy. I wasn't going to mess with that."

"Happy?" I laughed bitterly. "Your sources were wrong. It

didn't last with Ben. . . . You still never came back."

"I know. Things got pretty intense with the Destinos. Still are. But when I heard it might be Luke that was laundering the money, I got freaked. I knew you worked for him. I realized I had to reappear in your life even if the timing wasn't perfect."

I couldn't believe it. He'd planned to come back to me all this time. He'd never stopped wanting to be with me.

"I wish I could tell you I'm leaving the gang, but I can't. We've put everything we have into this operation and—"

I put a hand over his mouth. "I'm sick of hearing about them, okay? I'm done." I grabbed him, kissing him fiercely. He made a startled noise, but caught me around the waist, meeting my kiss and returning it, taking my tongue into his mouth.

Our mouths fused, our bodies drawn together like magnets. I broke off the kiss, breathing hard. "You saved yourself for me, so you're mine." I'd blurted out the words before realizing exactly what I was saying. But as his eyes narrowed in confusion, I knew I wasn't confused at all.

I wanted him. All of him. I couldn't even remember life before wanting him.

Mateo was my first love—my only love. This was my chance to be with him the way I'd always craved. I knew that if I didn't take this chance, *tonight*, I'd never have it again.

So what if we didn't have a future together? I wanted to be his first. I wanted him to feel my imprint on his soul forever. It would be a first for me, too—my first time being with someone I actually loved.

I stared into his eyes. "Come upstairs."

He was incredulous. "Are you sure?"

"I think we've earned this, haven't we?"

"God, yeah."

I went into his arms, and he kissed me like a drowning man desperate for air.

TEAM ME

MONDAY WAS JACKSON POLLOCK DAY at Compass.

It looked like a paint bomb had exploded everywhere.

Kylie was practically wearing a hazmat suit over her fabulous threads, including heavy-duty gloves to protect her manicure. I was wearing the usual ratty old T-shirt and shorts.

As I helped the kids with their paintings, I thought how funny it was that random drips and splotches could produce awesome artwork. The parents always got excited when it looked like their kids had done something genius.

"That's beautiful, Sofia." She sat quietly at my elbow, intensely focused on her painting. "Blue and orange is a great color combination."

Not quite a smile, but she seemed pleased.

"I can't believe you guys *did* it," Kylie said, her eyes wide. I couldn't have kept it from her. She saw it on my face the moment I walked in this morning. "I'm gonna have to get details."

"What did you guys do?" a paint-smeared Cameron asked.

"Played catch," Kylie said smoothly. "So, did Mateo catch the ball or fumble?"

My cheeks flushed. "There was some fumbling." To get our clothes off, I remembered. We'd been so eager, almost wild with wanting each other. The memories seared me.

"Whoa, that is epic! So what does this mean for you guys?"

"I think it meant good-bye."

"Excuse me?"

"He's not giving me what I need, so I'm not buying in. I can't. I want him in my life, but I don't *need* him."

I could see that more clearly than ever now. I wasn't going to accept him being in a gang. It would be so easy to throw caution aside and be with him. But I needed a guy who'd be there for me instead of running off doing gang business. I wouldn't settle, no matter how much I loved him. I was strong enough to stand on my own now. I'd proven it to myself time and again. I wasn't going to compromise for a guy—even Mateo.

"But don't you *love* him?"

"I love you, Kylie!" Cameron announced from across the table. "I love you in the morning and in the afternoon," he sang. "I love you in the evening and underneath the mooooon."

"I love you too, sweet pea," she said without taking her eyes off me.

"I do love him. But I told you, he's not ready to commit to a relationship." That was one way of putting it. I couldn't tell her the truth—that he was a Destino. I wished I could.

"It can't end this way!" Kylie pounded a fist on the table, spilling some paint.

"I didn't realize you were Team Mateo."

She scoffed. "I've never even met the guy. But based on everything you've said, I figured you guys were a done deal."

Cameron looked confused by the conversation. "What team are you on, Grace?"

"Team Me."

"Me too!" Cameron said. "Let's get her!" There was a sudden shriek as Cameron flung his paintbrush, which sprayed up into Kylie's face.

"Ugh!" Kylie shot to her feet. "I f-fink there's some paint in my mouff!" she sputtered.

"Sorry," Cameron said, looking crushed. "Sorry, Kylie. I'm just playing. Do you still love me?"

I could tell she *really* wanted to bitch at him, but she said, "Of courff."

She hurried off toward the bathroom.

Cameron giggled, the little bugger.

I wasn't sure if I felt more like throwing up or crapping my pants.

Either way, it wasn't going to be pretty.

The air was charged with electricity. I stood backstage with twenty-four poets from across Miami. God, had I actually wanted to be a finalist? This wasn't some campus café—it was a huge theater. The place was already packed.

The worst part was, there wasn't a podium for my cue card. Feenix had warned me about that. If I blanked out, I'd be screwed. So I'd memorized the hell out of my poem. I'd recited it in the shower, on the toilet, on the bus. I'd texted it to myself. I'd recited it while I was sleeping.

But that was no guarantee that I wouldn't forget the words.

If I did, my backup plan was to babble, babble, babble. Run.

Even Feenix "the Fenom" looked nervous. Instead of watching the other poets, she was sitting in a corner backstage, earbuds in.

It was a smart strategy. Watching the other poets kill it, one after the other, was only making me sick with nerves.

I knew I was out of my league here. I had no dreams of winning. My dream was to survive without humiliating myself. If I achieved that, I'd feel so light, I'd fly away.

I spotted Luke in the front row, a girl on either side of him. Nina and Jamar were also there. It was really nice of them to show up to support us, but they shouldn't have bothered. I was even more nervous in front of people I knew than people I didn't know.

Uh-oh. It was my turn.

I walked forward. My knees shook—could everyone tell? Thank God I'd made the last-minute decision to wear white sneakers instead of heels. I'd be poetic roadkill right now.

The thought made me laugh aloud as I approached the mike.

If I could just get the first words out, I'd have to trust that the rest would come. I opened my mouth.

Every bit of love
I have inside of me
Is an anchor around my neck
Pulling me under
The heaving waves
Dragging me into
Your murky depths.

Every bit of love
I have inside of me
Holds me down
To your bed of nails
Drops me over
The steep precipice,
Leaves me hanging
With no guardrail.

Every bit of love
I have inside of me
Is spreading slowly
Ending my life
If only I could free myself
Of these anchors
Break the surface
Maybe then
I'd breathe again.

I'd done it. *Yes.* My fist clenched with satisfaction.

Applause rose up around me, filling my ears. The next thing I knew, I was backstage and Feenix was hugging me.

"Mind blown!" she said.

"You listened?"

"Of course!"

"If it weren't for you, I would never have tried to do this."

"That makes me so happy." She smiled. "Hey, did you see Mateo here?"

"I . . ." My mouth opened. "I saw Luke and some people from work, but he wasn't sitting with them. Are you sure it was him?"

She nodded. "He was at the back. I don't think he meant for you to see him."

"Thanks for telling me." I was proud of what I'd done, and I knew he'd be proud of me. "Kill it, okay?"

"I will," she promised, then retreated back into her corner, popping in the earbuds.

I slipped out a stage door and went to the back of the theater, grabbing a seat in the last row. Scanning the vicinity, I realized that Mateo had already left. I guess he'd meant what he said: *I'll always be cheering you on from the sidelines, even if you don't know I'm there.*

Feenix went second to last. Since my own nerves were gone, I found myself getting nervous on her behalf. I knew she could do it. She was born for this.

But I also knew she'd be crushed if she didn't do well. A lot of people were expecting her to win.

Including me.

She walked out wearing one of Kenny's fedoras, a white cami, and baggy jeans. She was quiet for a moment, until the last of the whispers subsided and she knew we were in the palm of her hand.

I'm Feenix
As in, rising from the ashes.
I'm Feenix
As in, bless you.
I just wanted to say
By the way
That I'm biracial.
And I've been known to be
Bicurious
At least, at parties.
Not to mention
Bipolar
At least, when I'm hungry
Or having my period.
And possibly
Bicoastal
Or would be
If my dad kept in touch.
What I'm not
Is bipartisan

I take the side
Of the ninety-nine percent.
Those people who are struggling
I fight for them
Those who need food
Or can't pay the rent.
Yes, I'm Feenix
So nice to meet you
Now you know who I really am.
Part liberal
Part libertine
As for you?
I don't have a clue.

When it was over, the crowd roared. I jumped out of my seat, cheering.

I was pretty sure she smiled, though I was too far away to know for sure. But she must've known she'd nailed it.

She had it in the bag. At least, I hoped.

After the last performer, I went backstage to join the others as we waited for the winners to be announced.

Feenix hooked my arm in hers, bouncing in anticipation. Eventually the director of the whole thing got on stage. We closed our eyes as he announced the second and first runners-up.

"And the winner of the Miami Slam is Feenix Menzies!"

We jumped up and down. Someone grabbed her arm and pulled her onto the stage. She took a bow.

I lost track of Feenix after that. She was swarmed by well-wishers and local media. At the reception, I stood around for a while with Luke and my coworkers, then found a chance to slip out. I was exhausted, but happy exhausted, and ready to head home.

I went to the bus stop, sitting down on the bench. A familiar car pulled up. My heartbeat faltered. Mateo hadn't left. He'd been waiting for me this whole time.

He leaned his elbow out the window. "Congrats."

"I didn't win."

His mouth curved up. "So what? You did it."

I smiled, and we had a moment. "Yeah, I guess I did."

I got into the car, and he started to drive. "I was worried you'd go out partying with everybody."

"Nah. I was ready to call it a night." I glanced at him, felt a shiver go through me. I wasn't ready to anymore.

It had been more than two weeks since we'd last talked—and done far more than that. We'd hardly said a word to each other since. After we'd gotten so real that night, small talk seemed pointless.

There was a tight silence. He finally said, "I've been doing a lot of thinking."

"Famous last words." My insides got all twisted. He was making me hope again, damn him. "You're not going to ruin my night, are you? Because I'm feeling pretty high right now."

He glanced at me, smiling. "You were awesome up there. And no, I'm not going to ruin your night."

When we reached my place, he cut the engine and headlights. It was suddenly very dark, and the air in the car was thick. He hesitated, as if he expected me to invite him in. But I had no plan to do that.

"I made a decision. One you should know about."

My breath caught. "Are you leaving the gang?"

"Yes."

I blinked, afraid to believe it. My heart soared. "You're not kidding."

"No."

I fought the temptation to hurl myself into his arms. There had to be a catch. "Are they going to jump you out?"

He shook his head. "I told you, it's not that type of gang. We don't hurt each other. I won't say our leader wasn't pissed at my decision, but mostly because his girlfriend's gonna use it as ammo for *him* to move on too."

"Do you *want* to leave the gang?"

He let out a breath. "Those are my guys, Grace. In a lot of ways, they saved my life. But I want you more. I can't lose you again."

I chewed my lower lip. "That's how you feel *now*, but what about down the line? Are you going to hate me for making you leave them?"

"You're not making me leave. You walked away and gave me a chance to figure things out on my own. There's just one thing. I have to finish what I started. I'm close to finding out the truth about Luke. Once I do, I'm out."

"Oh." I deflated, but not completely. "How long will it be?"

"I don't know. Not very long."

I sighed. He was wrong about Luke, and if it took a few more weeks to realize it, that was fine with me. I squeezed his hand. "Do what you've gotta do."

"I will. Now I have to ask. Your poem, the anchors you were talking about . . ."

"I'm just trying to figure out how I can love someone without it hurting so much."

My mom. Dad. Alex. You.

"I'll show you how," he said, his eyes serious. He slid a hand behind my head and pulled me into him.

We kissed slowly, gently at first, but the need for each other simmered out of control. I broke away. "Tell me the moment you're out," I said. "Then we can be together for real."

His eyes were hooded with desire, but he nodded.

BLEEDING HEART

That boy sure has stinky socks! Good heavens!

I SMILED AT THE LATEST text from Carol Ann. The lady was a born nurturer, and Alex was her project. Strange how you could get to know someone through texting and email. Ever since Alex had moved in with her, we'd been in touch daily.

True to her word, she'd been looping me in on the wedding plans. First, she ran the venue by me—the Brookhaven Golf and Country Club—then she sent me color swatches and decor ideas from Pinterest. The process was fun. I could tell it was important for her to build a good relationship with me.

Dad had been smart to lock it down with Carol Ann. She

was Southern Baptist, and I had no doubt she'd made it clear that living in sin didn't fly with her. I was glad he'd stepped up.

I texted back:

You'd better buy some Febreze.

"Carol Ann is freaking hilarious," I said to Feenix, scrolling down through our last few texts and handing over my phone.

Feenix read one.

Made a cheese and crumb soufflé for Alex and your dad. Golly, those boys can inhale food!

Feenix looked at me. "Is this lady for real?"

I nodded.

She read some more texts, then handed back my phone. "Nice to see the wicked stepmom archetype isn't true. You've got yourself a Betty Crocker."

"Yeah." It was weird to think that eventually I'd be calling Carol Ann my stepmom. That would take some getting used to.

The late shows had all started, so the concession area was pretty quiet. I noticed Mateo hadn't been around for the last few minutes, which was odd because he was usually near the main entrance at this time.

Watching him was my addiction.

Watching him, knowing it wouldn't be too long now . . .

It was hard to stay away from each other, but I was sticking to my guns—we weren't getting together until he was 100 percent out of the gang. I'd waited four years for him, and I didn't want anything less than all of him.

He still drove me home. We talked in the car, laughed together, kissed, but it never went further than that. We were driving each other nuts. Sometimes he texted me in the middle of the night to tell me how much he wanted me.

The weird part was, I was in no rush. Two weeks had passed since the night of the city finals, and I was actually enjoying our state of limbo. I knew that once Mateo and I took that step, it would be for good. We'd been through our various hells and had come back to each other. Once he left the Destinos, I couldn't imagine anything that could keep us apart.

I went to the staff bathroom. On my way out, I thought I heard muffled shouting and scuffling.

There was a crash, as if a metal shelf had toppled over. Startled, I moved in the direction of the noise, toward the back storage room. Was a robbery going on? I doubted there was much in the storage room worth stealing.

A gunshot exploded.

My pulse kicked into overdrive. I ran to the concession area. Mateo wasn't there. I realized that whatever was happening in the storage room, he was probably in the middle of it.

What if he'd been shot? What if he was lying on the floor bleeding?

I turned around and headed down the hallway again. My hand shook as I reached for the door handle of the storage room, hearing the clanks and grunts from inside. There was a gunman in there. I was doing the opposite of what any sane person should do.

But I needed to know if Mateo needed help.

I swung open the door and my eyes swept the vast room. Chaos. Fighting.

It took me several seconds to figure out what was happening. Three guys in black masks were beating up two stocky bikers. My brain clued in to what the black masks meant—they must be Destinos.

Eddie was on the sidelines, holding his right arm, grimacing in pain. His glasses had been knocked off. He spotted me, and a look of relief came over his face. "Grace!" He hobbled toward me.

Eddie didn't make it any closer. Mateo came out of nowhere and grabbed him, hauling him away from me. "Don't get near her." Mateo turned to me. "According to the guys in the masks, he's been laundering money for those bikers."

Eddie was laundering the money? I stared at Eddie in disbelief. He might not be the most normal guy, but I never would've imagined he'd betray Luke. How could Eddie have possibly connected with the bikers?

I wanted to question Mateo, but I didn't trust myself to. I knew he was maintaining his cover, pretending not to know who the Destinos were, and I wouldn't do anything to jeopardize that. If the Brothers-in-Arms found out that he was the one behind this . . . I couldn't bear to think about it.

Something in Mateo's hand caught the light, and I looked down. He was holding a gun. "You should go," he said to me, over the shouts and fighting.

"But—" I said.

"Don't worry, everything's under control." Carefully, he unloaded the gun, then tucked it into his waistband, putting the bullets in his pocket.

I started to move toward the door, unsure of what to do. Eddie was slumped against the wall, moaning. "Grace, wait! You believe me, right? I don't know those bikers. Never seen them before in my life. I'm getting out of here." He struggled to get up, but Mateo shoved him back down.

"You should be helping me, Mateo!" Eddie shouted. "It's your job!"

"Shut up. I'm calling the cops." Mateo took out his phone and dialed 911. He pointed me toward the door, with a soundless *out*, then started speaking to the dispatcher. "This is the security guard at Cinema 1. We have a fight going on in the storage room at the back of the building. There are three guys in masks—they're pommeling two bikers. I think the bikers are Brothers-in-Arms based on the arm patches, but I'm no expert. Yeah, one of the bikers had a gun but I got it away from him. I don't know. Some type of deal was going down. Just get here as fast as you can."

Mateo's eyes were on the fight. The bikers were on the ground now, and the Destinos held them down as they zip-tied their hands. Instead of leaving the storage room, I slipped behind some cluttered metal shelves. I wasn't going to leave until this was over, until I was sure that Mateo didn't need me.

When Mateo got off the phone, Eddie started up again. "Please, you have to believe me! I got a call about a delivery. I came back here to Receiving to sign for it. Then I find myself face-to-face with those Brothers-in-whatever people. They scared the shit out of me! I didn't know what they were talking about! They just handed me this garbage bag and suddenly I'm getting attacked from all sides by guys in black masks. One of them broke my fucking arm! Go find out who he is so I can press charges!"

Mateo's face was grim. "I saw you try to hide the cash. What am I supposed to think?"

Eddie opened his mouth again to argue, but Mateo's icy

look shut him down. "Don't even bother. I'm calling Luke—he went out for a few minutes, but should be back any second." Mateo made the call. "You'd better get to the storage room right away. You'll see when you get here." He looked at Eddie. "Luke's in the parking lot. He'll be here in a minute."

Sweat dripped off Eddie's face. I could smell his desperation. "Luke'll believe me. He knows I'd never do what they're saying . . . it's total bullshit. Why would I launder money for a group of thugs? They're a menace to society, those people. I saw a documentary on them last—"

Eddie was still talking when Luke arrived.

Luke's eyes widened. "What the fuck?"

I could only imagine what Luke was thinking as he took in this scene. He saw the Destinos holding down the bikers. Saw the garbage bag open on the floor, rolls of cash spilling out. He saw Eddie, sweaty and pathetic.

Luke turned to Mateo, bewildered. "You gonna fill me in?"

Mateo was about to speak when one of the Destinos jogged over. A blue-eyed guy in a mask. I knew right away he was the guy who'd been at the hospital after Alex was hurt.

"Your employee here—" the Destino said, pointing down to Eddie, "has been laundering money through your business for the Brothers-in-Arms."

Mateo added, "I saw Eddie trying to hide the bag of cash."

"Sorry, can't stay," the Destino said. He and the two others ran out through the back door.

Stunned, Luke turned to Eddie.

"They've got it all backward," Eddie said. "I wasn't trying to hide any money. I don't even know who those biker people are! I have no clue what's—"

Luke cut him off. "Bull. *Shit*. After all I did for you!"

I'd seen Luke mad plenty of times, but never like this. The fury in his eyes was frightening. The person who'd helped him run his business, the person he'd taken under his wing, had betrayed him. I saw Mateo put a hand on his arm, as if afraid Luke would attack Eddie.

But Luke didn't move. He just stared at him.

That's when the cops came to break up the party.

Later that night, Mateo and I sprawled on the couch. I had no intention of letting go of him. The sound of that gunshot echoed through my head, making me squeeze him tighter.

"Turns out I was right—Luke's not guilty after all," I said, lifting my head from his chest. "If that sounds like *I told you so*, it is."

He smirked. "Yeah, you told me so. Maybe those instincts of yours are trustworthy after all. Who knew?"

I smacked his arm. "You should've listened to me."

"Believe it or not, I did." He sobered. "Luke was the obvious suspect, but you got me wondering if there was anyone else with enough access to do it. The only person was Eddie. So I started watching him closely. Turned out that sometimes, when Luke wasn't around, he'd meet a couple of the Brothers at the back door to take in the cash. He'd add it to the daily numbers, launder it using two accounts under the theater's name, then cut checks to the Brothers through an offshore account."

I flashed back to Eddie stumbling toward me. He looked so desperate. "An offshore account? That sounds pretty sophisticated. I can't believe he pulled it off."

"We all know Eddie's a smart guy. But not smart enough to stay away from cocaine."

I frowned. "What?"

"Eddie's an addict. He hides it well. Luke knows but has always tried to help him. Once I found out about the coke problem, it all started to make sense. Eddie must've been getting his coke from the Brothers-in-Arms. He probably owed them more money than he could ever pay, and they used that to force him to launder their money through the theater."

I felt sad for Eddie. It was one thing to commit a crime out of greed, but another to do it because you're trapped.

"The cops have been building a case against the Brothers-in-Arms for years," he said. "Eddie could help them get their convictions. He just has to cooperate."

"And if he doesn't?"

"Then he'll go to prison. If that happens, my guess is the Brothers will have him killed. He's too much of a wild card for them to do anything else. Eddie's only real choice is to testify against the Brothers and get the hell out of town. If he's lucky, the cops might give him a protection deal."

"You mean witness protection?"

"Yeah. He'll have a chance to start over. He'd be smart to take it." Mateo looked at me. "Eddie probably thinks his life is over, but it doesn't have to be. He can avoid prison and move on. It's not like he murdered someone."

He was silent for a while, and I knew he was thinking about his brother.

"Maybe you should write to him," I said. "To Mig, I mean. You've got nothing to lose."

"Don't I? If I write to him, it'll feel like . . . like I'm letting him back in. I'm not sure I can do that."

"Because he might hurt you again."

"Maybe."

"Do you think you'll ever forgive him?"

He sighed. "Forgiveness is a gift you give yourself—that's what they say, right? It's about letting go of the anger? Well, I'm not there yet. Don't know if I'll ever be."

"I don't think you need to forgive him to write him a letter."

He exhaled. "I wish I could do it for my mom. It would

make her happy." Warmth entered his eyes. "I'm starting to wonder if your bleeding heart is contagious."

I placed a hand on his chest, feeling the steady thump of his heart. "I'm sorry to say, yours is just as bleeding."

Mateo had joined the Destinos because he wanted to help people and had become a paramedic for the same reason. Despite everything he'd been through, Mateo had never lost the kindness that made me fall for him in the first place.

"Your investigation is over," I said. "It's in the cops' hands now. So that means you're out of the gang, right?"

"Yeah." He wrapped his arms around me. "I can't tell you how long I've waited to be with you. I don't think I could get through one more day without you."

"You won't have to." I grabbed his hair and kissed him, gently biting his bottom lip. "Your ass is mine, Lopez."

He laughed. "Everything I have is yours."

I smiled against his mouth. "I love you."

"I love you too."

It occurred to me that maybe it made sense after all—life, that is, the wonder and the suckage. Maybe we all find our way to where we need to be. I was sure there was a poem in there somewhere. But I'd have to write it another time.

FIREBALL

TEN DAYS LATER, I STOOD in my bedroom, excitement pumping through me.

One hour and forty-seven minutes until Pitbull.

I double-checked my purse for the tickets and backstage passes.

Nervousness shot through me. Would I actually get to meet him? Would I be able to speak without getting tongue-tied?

The doorbell rang. I went downstairs and looked through the peephole. With a gasp, I opened the door.

Alex stood there with a crooked smile and a backpack slung over his shoulder. "Hey, Grace."

I yanked him inside, throwing my arms around him.

"What the hell are you doing here?"

"I thought it would be cool to surprise you. There was a seat sale on JetBlue. So here I am."

"This is awesome! How long are you staying?"

"About that. Hang on, I'm starving." Alex dropped his backpack, washed his hands in the kitchen sink, then grabbed a bag of chips from the cupboard. "I'm just here a couple of days to pack up my stuff," he said between chips. "I've decided to stay in Atlanta. It's really—" He stopped crunching. "I'm sorry. I didn't mean to upset you."

"You're not." My eyes had misted up, but not from sadness. "I think you've got a good thing going there."

"I'm glad you're cool with it." Smiling, he ate some more chips. "It's a sweet city. Better than Miami. The people are so chill. Everybody here's always stressing, looking for drama."

"It's the right decision." I'd been hoping he would stay in Atlanta. He'd have parents there, and could start fresh at a new school in the fall. He wouldn't have to be looking over his shoulder.

"I know you'll miss me, since I was so great to live with," he said wryly.

There wasn't much I could say to that. He'd made my life hell over the past year. I went over and hugged him. I had no doubt that Mom would be happy with his decision.

"Dad wants to know if you still want to live in this house," he said. "Maybe he'll sell it and use some of the money to help you rent a place."

I looked around. I'd thought about it too. It would be painful to leave this house and all its memories, but it might be the right thing. "It's too much space for just me. I'll talk to him about it. Maybe I'll find an apartment near campus."

"Makes sense. So what's your plan tonight?" Alex asked. "I've been craving Rico's Pizza, I won't lie. That's the only thing that pisses me off about Atlanta—the pizza. It's the thin, wood-fired oven kind. Now the ribs and fried chicken, they're ridiculous."

"Actually . . . I'm going out tonight." I hadn't told him about the Pitbull concert. I'd been planning on telling him after the fact. I knew he'd be upset to miss it, and if I told him about the backstage passes, he'd freak. "Hang on. Let me make a call."

He put up a hand. "You don't have to change your plans for me. I knew you'd have stuff going on. Plus, I gotta pack up all my stuff."

"I know, but just wait a minute."

I grabbed my phone, went upstairs and called Mateo.

"Ready when you are," he answered.

"You're gonna hate me, but there's been a change of plans."

"Don't tell me you've decided to take Luke instead," he said, but I heard the laughter in his voice.

"It's just that Alex is in town."

There was a pause. "Are you serious?"

"Yeah. He came home to pack his things. Just showed up at the door. You know how he worships Pitbull. It's a serious obsession for him. I'd like to bring him if you're okay with it."

"Of course, but . . . I don't think it's a good idea for him to go out in public."

"We've got box seats. There are going to be thousands of people there. What are the chances anyone he knows will spot him, much less one of the Locos? I think it's okay. Don't you?"

He hesitated. "I guess. Just promise me you'll stay in the box and won't go wandering all over the place."

"Of course not. Box, then backstage. That's it."

"All right. I'll drop you guys off. See you soon." He hung up.

I went back into the living room where Alex was watching TV. "Plans have changed. You're coming with me."

"Where we going?"

I went over to my purse, pulled out the tickets and back-stage passes. "Want to go see Mr. Worldwide?"

Alex's eyes bulged, and he leaped off the couch. "Are you kidding me?"

An hour later, Mateo showed up. Alex and I hopped into his car.

"Mateo!" Alex said. "How's it going?"

"All right—other than the fact that you stole my date."

Mateo backed out of the driveway. "How's Atlanta treating you?"

"It's a sick place. I've got lots to tell you. We'll hang out after the concert, right?"

"Definitely. I'll pick you guys up. Does anybody know you're in town?"

"Just Dad and Carol Ann."

"Good."

If Mateo thought it was a real risk, he would've argued with me. According to his friend the snitch, there was no campaign to find Alex these days. The Locos had bigger problems right now: the Destinos.

"How's life as a paramedic?" Alex asked.

"Intense. You learn a lot on the job that you never learned in school. I'm still considered a trainee for the first few months, but I'm getting paid now."

"That's cool. I'm gonna be getting paid too. I got a job at the gym where I do mixed martial arts. I'll be working at the front desk, giving out towels and answering the phone."

"You didn't tell me that!" I said, turning back to look at him.

"I just got the call yesterday. I start next week. I'll even get a free membership."

"It'll feel good to have some cash flow," Mateo said. "You'll see."

Mateo dropped us off a short time later, as close to the gates as he could get. He tossed Alex a black-and-orange Orioles cap. "Wear this. Remember, go right to the box. Text me half an hour before you want a pickup. I don't want you waiting out in the open. I'll text you when I get here."

"Thanks," I said. "We'll be careful."

"Hey, Alex," Mateo said, over his shoulder. "If Pitbull makes a move on your sister, tell him she's taken."

Alex grinned. "Sure."

I laughed, giving Mateo a kiss before shutting the door.

God, I loved him.

Our seats were in a swanky box with cushy, movie-theater-style chairs. A rich-looking family was in there with us—two parents, a glamorous dark-haired girl of about sixteen, four of her fancy friends, and a boy who looked about ten. He was playing a game on his iPad, scowling as if he didn't want to be there.

Alex and I claimed our seats in the front corner of the box and looked at each other, bursting with excitement.

A waiter came in. He took a long order from the family, then approached us, asking if we'd like drinks or food.

"Is it free?" I asked quietly.

The waiter nodded. "Included in your ticket price."

"I'll have a hot dog," Alex said. "And a beer."

The waiter lifted an eyebrow.

"Okay, Pepsi then."

"Diet 7UP and a bag of chips," I said.

When the waiter left, Alex looked out across the packed stadium. "I can't believe this! How much did you pay for the tickets?"

"Nothing. My boss gave them to me."

"Are you serious?"

"Yep."

He looked puzzled. "Did you have to sleep with him or something?"

"No, he's not like that." I smirked. "His friend is running security here, so he got them free. He knows I'm Pitbull-obsessed."

The stadium lights went down, and the stage lit up. We had an incredible view. Thousands of people suddenly hushed.

When Nayer appeared on stage in a flowing Cleopatra-style gown, illuminated by dozens of white lights, Alex jumped out of his seat and whooped for joy. He worshipped Nayer and had a poster of her in a leather bathing suit on his bedroom wall. She'd recorded a few songs with Pitbull and was from Miami too, so it was no surprise that she was opening for him.

Alex watched, riveted, salivating over his dream girl.

We cheered and danced.

When Nayer sang "Suavemente," Mohombi joined her on stage, giving the females in the stadium some eye candy.

Pitbull came out, rapping his part of the song. We hollered our heads off. I'd have no voice tomorrow, but it was worth it.

Next, Pitbull performed "Give Me Everything," and Nayer joined him. Mohombi sang Ne-Yo's part. It was one of my all-time favorite songs. Alex and I went wild, dancing and screaming.

I looked over at Alex and felt a surge of happiness. Was I really at a Pitbull concert with my brother? Had we actually become friends? After everything that had happened this past year, it was a miracle. I blinked back tears.

When "Fireball" came on, we lost our minds. Alex got up on his seat and pumped his arms. I felt a tap on my leg. It was the scowling boy with the iPad. He pointed to the Jumbotron.

Alex was on the huge screens, dancing like a crazy person.

"Get down!" I grabbed Alex's arm and yanked him to his seat. "Camera's on you!"

He sat down quickly, pulling the ball cap over his eyes. Within seconds, the camera had focused on a group of blondes in bikini tops.

"How long was I on?" Alex asked, dashing sweat from his forehead.

"I have no idea. Probably just a few seconds." No need to panic, I told myself. But my pulse was racing.

Alex didn't look troubled at all. In fact, he was grinning.

The next hour was a blur of awesomeness.

Pitbull gave a grand bow after his last song and walked offstage. But the whole stadium cheered him back on. *"Pit-bull! Pit-bull!"* Thousands of stomping feet made the stadium shake.

I touched Alex's shoulder. "We should head backstage now."

"But he's gonna do another song!"

"We can beat the crowd. I want to make sure we actually get to meet him."

"Good point."

He followed me out of the box. We heard the crowd go ballistic as Pitbull came back onstage. I hated to miss the last song, but it was worth it if we got to meet him. Backstage passes were never a guarantee, and we had no idea how many people had them.

I didn't know where the backstage area was, so I asked a security guard and he gave us directions. "Down the hall over there. Just follow the twists and turns until the end. There'll be a sign."

We hurried down the twisting hallway, laughing like little kids. It took a whole five minutes to reach the end of the hall, but once we did, we knew we'd arrived at the right place. The sign said: "Secured Backstage Area. Passes Only." There was a security guard with a red badge around his neck.

We held out our backstage passes.

He took a careful look, then nodded. "You'll be first in line. It's your lucky day."

We glanced at each other in disbelief. Meeting Pitbull was our dream, and it was coming true.

We were in a high-ceilinged area that looked like a large, mostly empty stockroom. Heavy doors and black curtains separated us from the real backstage area. I could hardly keep still as we waited. Gradually, more fans joined us. The room buzzed with anticipation.

Pitbull appeared. It was like something out of a dream, with everything going into slow motion. Alex and I were told to move up. We were standing just five feet away from Mr. Worldwide himself. I was having heart palpitations.

Pitbull wore his trademark white suit. He was sweaty from the performance, laughing with his security guards about something.

He was beautiful.

One of the security guards, a heavyset black guy, curled his finger at Alex and me. We approached Pitbull. "Hey, there," he said with a dazzling smile.

Oh my God!

We both said hi.

My phone was trembling. Or my hand was trembling. Could I do it? Ask for a picture?

"You were amazing," I managed to say. "Just amazing!" I sounded like an ass, but he didn't seem to mind.

"Sickest concert ever!" Alex said.

Pitbull's grin melted me. "I aim to please. How about a picture?"

He'd read my mind! Or maybe it was what everybody wanted. Still. "That would be great," I said, looking down at my phone. A text from Mateo was on the screen.

911. Locos know you're there. Find cops and stay with them.

I dropped my phone. It smacked the cement floor.

This couldn't be happening. This had to be a nightmare.

I turned to Alex. "We have to go."

Alex looked at me like I was crazy. "But don't you want a pic?"

Pitbull frowned, more perceptive than my brother. "Is everything okay, honey?"

"The Locos are coming for you!" I shouted at Alex. His eyes went huge.

We had to run.

I spotted an emergency exit at the far end of the room. If we ran out there, there would likely be cops nearby. I'd spotted plenty of them earlier.

"That way," I said to Alex.

My heart stopped.

Too late.

They'd found us.

A group of four Locos blew past the security guard at the room's entrance. The guard shouted, running after them.

The Locos paid no attention—they were fixated on Alex.

They came at him like a car crash, fists flying. I screamed. I lunged at one of the guys who was attacking Alex, kicking, biting. A fist flew into my face, and I stumbled back, tasting blood.

The scene was like something out of a nightmare. Several feet away, Pitbull's two security guys were hauling him away. Pitbull was struggling to get away from them, shouting at them. In a flash of awareness, I knew Pitbull had realized that the threat wasn't against him, but us—but his security hadn't figured it out.

Alex was on the floor, not moving. A huge Loco threw him over his shoulder.

"Noooo!" I screamed.

The Locos hustled him toward the back of the room, blasting through the emergency exit. Alarms went off. I ran after them, screaming with everything I had. One of them turned and grabbed me so tightly his fingernails cut into my skin.

Animale.

His green eyes met mine. "Santo's getting his. Ain't nothing you can do about it."

I struggled in his grip, kicking at his shins. He shook his head, unimpressed. Behind him, I saw Alex get dumped in the trunk of a red sports car.

"*Hasta luego*, Grace," Animale said with a smile. He jumped into the front seat and the car sped off.

I ran after it. It got farther and farther away, but I kept running. It was weaving around other cars, trying to get out of the crowded parking lot.

A horn blared, and brakes squealed behind me.

Mateo.

"The red car," I shouted. "He's in the trunk!"

Mateo nodded and floored the gas.

I stopped running. I hugged myself as my insides broke apart. They were planning to kill Alex. There was no doubt in my mind. And I was powerless to stop them.

Mateo was blasting through the parking lot, dodging cars, people, gathering speed. He was Alex's only chance.

A strange stillness came over me. After all Alex and I went through, was this how it was going to end? After he'd changed his life, were the Locos going to end it?

I watched, heart in my throat, as Mateo gained on the red

sports car. Somehow, he'd almost caught up to them. But the Locos were about to clear the parking lot and turn onto the highway. If they made it to the busy highway, the chances of Mateo catching them were almost nonexistent.

He wasn't going to let that happen.

A huge crashing sound rang out as Mateo rammed the back of the sports car at full speed.

The Locos spun out, smashing into a traffic light pole. I stared in wordless horror as Mateo's car careened onto its left side, then flipped once, twice.

I ran toward the crash scene. The concrete of the parking lot stretched before me for what seemed like miles. My feet simply couldn't run any faster, but I kept going. I had to get to them.

Mateo's car exploded.

Noooo!

A cloud of fire spurted up from Mateo's car.

I stumbled forward, my feet bloodied, sweat dripping into my eyes. By the time I reached the scene, there were several cop cars, ambulances. A crowd had gathered. I tried to push through it, but a police officer thrust me away. "Stay back!"

I found another way through the crowd and ran up to an ambulance just as they were closing its back doors.

"Who's in there?" I asked desperately, but the paramedic

ignored me and jumped into the driver's seat. He drove off, blaring the siren.

More ambulances were coming. I saw stretchers. One guy was covered in blood. I didn't even know who—

"Grace!"

Alex's arms went around me. He gripped me tight, sobbing into my shoulder. "They told me they were g-gonna kill me."

I pulled away. "Where's Mateo? Did you see him? Did he get out?"

He looked confused. "Mateo? What do you mean?"

"He's the one who crashed into you!" I shouted. "He's the one who stopped them!"

"I'm right here," came a voice from behind me.

I turned, and my knees almost buckled with relief. Blood dripped from a gash in Mateo's forehead.

"You got out!" I sobbed into his chest.

His face was buried in my hair. "I told you, when your engine's busted, you have to get outta there."

Alex's arms were around us both now. He was crying and thanking Mateo over and over. Mateo eventually pulled away and told him to calm down. "We have to deal with the cops and make sure those bitches get put away for what they did. Do you hear me?"

"Okay." But Alex was shaking. "A-Animale said he was gonna cut—"

"Animale is dead," Mateo told him. "He went through the windshield."

"Oh." Alex's expression went from horror to relief. "Oh."

I had the giggles.

It might be strange to have the giggles on the most traumatic day of your life, especially in the waiting room of a police station. But there it was.

Although Alex, Mateo, and I had given our statements hours ago, the cops wanted us to stick around. We were hoping it wasn't because they were planning to arrest Mateo. He'd explained why he had to ram the car. There must be enough witnesses for the cops to put together what had happened.

As we sat there, Alex scrolled through the headlines on his phone. Apparently the incident had made national news.

"Kidnapping at Pitbull Concert"

"Pitbull Caught in Gang Vendetta"

TMZ posted pictures of Pitbull, wide-eyed, being dragged away from the fight by his security guards.

I giggled.

Mateo looked at me with concern, but I showed him the pictures, and he admitted it was sort of funny.

When Alex got up to use the bathroom, I asked Mateo, "Are you okay?"

"I'm fine."

I could see that he wasn't fine. He must be as shaken up as Alex and me, he just dealt with it in a quieter, saner way.

He sighed. "I should've stopped you from taking Alex to the concert. It seemed like such a small risk."

"Don't blame yourself. It was my call. I didn't think there was any chance that a Loco would spot us with thousands of people there. I hadn't counted on Alex being on the Jumbotron."

But that, according to the Loco snitch, was how we'd been spotted. Animale and his friends had been at the concert and had seen Alex on the screens. Animale had texted other Locos, bragging that he was finally going to get his revenge. Someone must have followed us from the box to the backstage area, then gone to get the others as we'd waited for Pitbull. It all went wrong for us—except one thing.

"You got there in time," I said, squeezing his hand. "That's all that matters."

"I was already in my car heading to the concert when the snitch called me. From the second I dropped you off, it didn't feel right." He looked grim. "I regret letting you guys go to the concert. But I don't regret that Animale is dead."

It couldn't be easy, knowing he'd been responsible for another person's death. But Animale had intended to kill Alex. For most of the Locos, dealing with Alex was a matter of gang business. For Animale, it was personal. I'd seen the evil in his eyes. Alex would never have been safe with Animale looking for him.

When Alex returned from the bathroom, we went back to looking at the news headlines.

Shouting erupted near the entrance of the police station, and we all looked up. Pitbull and his security team were striding through the automatic doors. Paparazzi swarmed but couldn't set foot in the police station.

Pitbull wore a white pinstripe shirt, open at the collar in a V, and a loose tie. He caught sight of us and did a double take. "You two okay?"

We nodded.

"Good. Some crazy shit back there, huh?" Pitbull and his crew followed an officer down a hall.

Mateo's arm tightened around me. I snuggled into him.

A while later, Mateo's blue-eyed friend showed up—he'd been disappearing and reappearing all night. He was the Destino named X that Mateo had told me about.

"Pitbull and his bodyguards backed you up," X said, sitting down next to us. "It's all good."

Mateo looked relieved. The pieces were falling into place. The cops knew he'd caused the crash to save Alex.

But there was something else too.

Mateo was a Destino—or had been until recently. I bet the word of a Destino meant something to the cops. I didn't quite understand it, but it seemed the Destinos and the cops had . . . not a partnership, but an understanding.

"The Locos who attacked you will be facing multiple charges, maybe even conspiracy to murder," X said to Alex. "Hope you'll be ready to testify."

Alex nodded. "I want to see them put away."

"Good," X said with a faint smile.

A while later, one of Pitbull's security guys came up to us. "This is yours, right?" He held out my phone. "Pitbull wanted you to have it back."

The glass face was broken, but I was glad to have it. "Please tell him thanks."

Looking down at the phone, I pressed the button to see if it still worked—and it turned on, thankfully. On the screen, there was a new background photo. It was a picture of Pitbull. He'd taken a selfie, doing a peace sign.

Mateo looked at me. "What is it?"

I handed him the phone, dissolving in laughter.

THE WEDDING

(Four months later)

FALL IN ATLANTA WAS BREATHTAKING. Red and gold leaves covered the grounds of the golf course. As we made our way up the sidewalk toward Dad and Carol Ann's wedding reception, my eyes drank in the scenery—and Mateo. He looked incredible in the charcoal suit he'd borrowed from a friend.

"You clean up nice, Lopez," I said.

"Thanks." He shrugged. "The arms of this suit are a little short, but it's good enough."

"This is such a pretty place, isn't it?"

He stopped walking and admired the scenery, inhaling the fresh air. "Pretty, yeah." He turned to me, eyes warm. "Absolutely gorgeous."

I hugged him. "I'm so glad you could be here."

"I told you I would be. Did you doubt me?"

"No." But I knew it was no small feat for a rookie paramedic to get out of working a holiday weekend. "What'd you promise Devin to take your shifts?"

"Cash."

"You *paid* him?"

He nodded, smiling down at me. "It was worth it."

Yes, it was. This was a big day for my family—and he was part of us now. He had to be here.

I took a deep, shuddering breath, and he asked, "Nervous?"

"A little. I hope they like my poem."

"They'll love it."

"I hope I don't start to cry when I'm delivering it."

"Cry if you want. Isn't that what people do at weddings?"

"Good point." I bit my lip. "I'm not sure I'm any good at writing love poetry, though. I'm better at the dark, angsty stuff."

He laughed down at me. "You'll have to get used to the happy stuff."

We headed inside. My eyes swept the room, and I knew Carol Ann would be pleased. The dining room was lit with candle sconces, throwing amber light across the tables. I caught the scent of flowers and forest. Touches of Carol Ann's crafts were everywhere—in the autumn-inspired centerpieces, in the painted name blocks on each table with words like *LOVE*, *FOREVER*, and *BELIEVE*.

Mateo and I sat down at table one, next to the head table at the front of the room. Alex was already there. His head was bent as he texted someone.

"Let me guess—Britney?" I asked.

"Yeah. So?"

"Who's Britney?" Mateo asked.

"Alex's girlfriend."

"She's just a friend," Alex said. A sly grin came to his lips. "For now, anyway."

"Nice," Mateo said.

"Want to send her a pic of you looking all dapper?" I asked.

"Good idea." Alex handed me his phone and posed, looking ultracool.

He approved the photo and sent it. A moment later he said, "She says I look so cute. *Cute?*"

"It's girl-speak for hot, trust me," I said, patting his hand.

Alex's world was pretty damned good these days. He'd enrolled in the neighborhood high school and had already found a group of friends. His marks were higher than I'd ever seen them, thanks to Carol Ann's help. I could never thank her enough for everything she'd done for him.

A lot had changed in the last few months. Within days of putting our house up for sale, it had sold. We'd scrambled to pack things up before the closing date. I'd moved into off-campus housing with two girls in my program, and we got along great, although I didn't know them well yet. Between school, work, and spending time with Mateo, I wasn't home very much.

A brunette in a blue satin dress went up to the podium. "Good evening, everyone! I'm Carol Ann's friend Julie, and I'll be your emcee tonight. Now, why don't we extend a warm welcome to the wedding party?"

The song "Celebrate!" blared from the speakers and we all stood up as Fay and Don, Carol Ann's sister and her husband, entered the dining room. Everybody cheered as they went up to the head table. They were the ones who'd set Dad and Carol Ann up in the first place.

Our cheers reached a crescendo as the newlyweds came in. They looked so bouncy and excited, I had to laugh. Dad even pumped his fist as they jogged across the room, hand in hand, and plunked down at the head table, breathless.

Behind the podium, Julie turned to me. "And now Marc's daughter, Grace, has a poem for us."

Smoothing my red strapless dress, I walked up to the mike.

I looked out at the expectant faces, then at my dad. He was bright-eyed and smiling. It hit me that I hadn't seen him happy in so long that I'd forgotten what it looked like. I realized that I wasn't just happy for him and for Carol Ann, but for Mom. She'd be glad he'd found someone to share his life with.

Tears came to my eyes, clouding my vision. I blinked them back, took a deep breath, and leaned toward the mike.

Their love
Was a brilliant beacon
That carried them to shore

Their words
A gentle promise
Binding them forevermore

Their vow
As he held her hand
Was a pledge for all their days

Their future
Spread out before them
Full of love, now and always.

Everybody clapped. Dad and Carol Ann got up and hugged me. I hugged them back, because I'd meant every word.

Once the dinner and speeches were over, the bride and groom danced to "I'm into Something Good" by Herman's Hermits. Then the DJ pumped up the party. The dance floor filled up fast. When Pitbull came on, I looked at Alex. He raised a brow, as if to say, *Should we show them how it's done?*

We hit the dance floor, and did just that.

When the DJ put on a slow song, Mateo joined me on the dance floor. We swayed together, looking into each other's eyes. I had a flash of the future—a gut feeling that one day we'd be dancing at our own wedding.

"What's got you smiling?" he asked.

"You."

"Me?"

"Well, actually you and me."

He said into my ear, "You and me right now? Or last night?"

I thought about last night, about those hungry hours together, and my whole body heated up. "Neither. I was thinking of you and me . . . in the future."

He drew back, and his face was serious. "I think about that too."

We had a moment. There was nothing like having a moment with Mateo, when the love passed between us, when words weren't necessary.

We pulled each other close, and I leaned my head against his chest as we moved to the music. *This*, right here, was bliss.

When the song ended, the dancing fired up again. We went outside for a break and a breath of air. The sun had set and the stars had come out. It was so rare that I was far enough away from a city to see the stars.

"I took your suggestion," he said into the darkness.

"Which one?"

"I finally wrote Mig."

That was good news, but it must have been tough for him to reach out to his brother. "Tell me about it."

"I told him about my daily life, just like he does in his letters. I told him some of the crazy stuff I deal with at work. About you. I wanted him to know things are going good for me, but not rub it in his face."

"Did he write back yet?"

"Yeah. At the start of the letter he went off on me for not writing sooner, but then he said he wanted to hear more paramedic stories. He read some of them to his cellmates. And he said he was so bored that he decided to do his GED. Maybe even take some college courses after that."

"Really? He used to hate school."

"Yeah, and get this—he's been taking yoga every week. It's part of some new program to teach the inmates mindfulness."

"Wow." I tried to see the expression on his shadowed face. "I'm glad you wrote to him."

"Me too." He put his arms around me. "I thought maybe if I act like I forgive him, it'll sink in somehow. He's my brother— I have to try. And my mom was really happy about it."

"I admire you, Mateo." He was choosing to be there for his brother regardless of whether or not Mig deserved it. I remembered my mom's words, *Love's never wasted.* A sense of comfort washed over me. Love wasn't just a feeling, it was a choice. Mom had figured that out long ago. Mateo had too.

"Your necklace is sparkling," he said.

Finally. "I was wondering if you'd ever notice." I lifted up the little ring dangling from the silver chain. "Recognize it?"

His eyes narrowed as he studied it. "No way. Is that the promise ring I gave you?"

I nodded.

"I can't believe you kept it."

My fingers caressed the smooth silver ring. "I won't lie—I wanted to throw it away many times. But I couldn't shake the feeling that I needed to keep it just in case."

"In case what?"

"In case you decided to keep your promise to be with me forever."

He looked down at me, and I saw the love glittering in his eyes. "I'm keeping that promise."

"Good." I slid my arms around his neck, pulling him down to me. "I'm holding you to it."

GREAT BOOKS BY
ALLISON
VAN DIEPEN

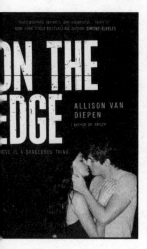

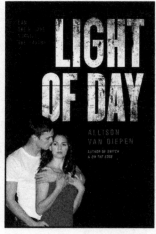

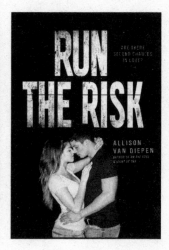